"You know all about pain, don't you, Alex?"

He kept his head down, his hair shining in the candlelight from their dinner table.

Tabitha pressed on. "Losing someone doesn't mean you can't rejoin the human race."

"I've already done that."

"Have you, Alex? Have you dated? Kissed a woman? Had sex? Those are normal functions of a human, aren't they?"

He looked up then and his gaze seemed to burn into her. She could feel her body temperature rising with every passing second. "Why do you care, Tabitha?" he asked in a husky voice. "Are you offering?"

Dear Reader,

Four special women shatter the barricades they've built around their dreams, in Silhouette Romance this month. Be it openly defying the life role set out for them or realizing their life's ambition, these independent ladies represent the type of aspirational heroines we're looking for in Silhouette Romance.

Myrna Mackenzie launches our newest trilogy, SHAKESPEARE IN LOVE, with *Much Ado About Matchmaking* (SR #1786) in which a woman who doesn't think she's special or beautiful enough for the worldly hero finally gets the courage to listen to her heart. *The Texan's Suite Romance* (SR #1787) rounds out Judy Christenberry's LONE STAR BRIDES continuity and features a woman who knows Mr. Right when she meets him but now must help him heal enough to let love back into his lonely life. When her screenplay is made into a movie set on her family's ranch, one woman thinks she's fulfilled all her dreams...until she meets one very handsome stuntman. Watch this drama unfold in *Lights, Action...Family!* (SR #1788)—the concluding romance in Patricia Thayer's LOVE AT THE GOODTIME CAFÉ miniseries. Finally, Crystal Green wraps up the BLOSSOM COUNTY FAIR series with *Her Gypsy Prince* (SR #1789) in which a sheltered woman bucks her family's wishes to pursue a forbidden love.

And be sure to come back next month when Elizabeth Harbison puts a modern spin on Shakespeare's *Taming of the Shrew.*

Happy reading,

Ann Leslie Tuttle
Associate Senior Editor

Please address questions and book requests to:
Silhouette Reader Service
U.S.: 3010 Walden Ave., P.O. Box 1325, Buffalo, NY 14269
Canadian: P.O. Box 609, Fort Erie, Ont. L2A 5X3

JUDY
Christenberry

The Texan's Suite
Romance

Lone Star
Brides

SILHOUETTE **Romance** ®
Published by Silhouette Books
America's Publisher of Contemporary Romance

SILHOUETTE BOOKS

ISBN 0-373-19787-X

THE TEXAN'S SUITE ROMANCE

Copyright © 2005 by Judy Christenberry

Printed in U.S.A.

Books by Judy Christenberry

Silhouette Romance

The Nine-Month Bride #1324
*Marry Me, Kate #1344
*Baby in Her Arms #1350
*A Ring for Cinderella #1356
†Never Let You Go #1453
†The Borrowed Groom #1457
†Cherish the Boss #1463
**Snowbound Sweetheart #1476
Newborn Daddy #1511
When the Lights Went Out… #1547
**Least Likely To Wed #1570
Daddy on the Doorstep #1654
**Beauty & the Beastly Rancher #1678
**The Last Crawford Bachelor #1715
Finding a Family #1762
††The Texan's Reluctant Bride #1778
††The Texan's Tiny Dilemma #1782
††The Texan's Suite Romance #1787

*The Lucky Charm Sisters
†The Circle K Sisters
**From the Circle K
††Lone Star Brides

Silhouette Books

The Coltons
The Doctor Delivers

A Colton Family Christmas
"The Diplomat's Daughter"

Lone Star Country Club
The Last Bachelor

JUDY CHRISTENBERRY

has been writing romances for over fifteen years because she loves happy endings as much as her readers do. She's a bestselling author for Harlequin American Romance, but she has a long love of traditional romances and is delighted to tell a story that brings those elements to the reader. A former high school French teacher, Judy devotes her time to writing. She hopes readers have as much fun reading her stories as she does writing them. She spends her spare time reading, watching her favorite sports teams and keeping track of her two adult daughters.

Chapter One

Tabitha Tyler woke slowly. It was the first day of summer vacation, a day she'd dreamed of for several months now. She'd planned a day with no problems, no mustdos. Just peace and quiet.

The ringing phone shattered the stillness. She looked at her watch automatically. Nine-thirty. It must be one of her sisters. Had Tommie, the oldest of the triplets, gone into an early labor? Tabitha grabbed the phone.

"Hello?"

"Tabitha, it's Mona."

Mona Langston had been Tabitha's publicist when last year she launched her exercise videos aimed at teenagers, the age level to whom Tabitha taught P.E. in school. They'd become good friends.

"You don't sound so good, Mona. What's wrong?"

"I'm in the hospital. I've been in a car wreck." Before Tabitha could inquire, she added, "Both my legs are broken."

"Oh, Mona, I'm so sorry. Is there anything I can do?"

"I was hoping you'd ask. Tabitha, I have a new client who is moving me into the big time. His publisher recommended me because of the feedback from your tour we did last summer."

"Congratulations, Mona, but that doesn't tell me what I can do."

"Think about it. I can't take this guy on tour. And I'm a one-woman office. I don't have anyone to replace me."

"Is there any way you can delay the tour?"

"No! We're supposed to leave tomorrow and be on the road for six weeks. It's all planned. All you'd have to do is confirm the arrangements and have him follow the plan. You could do it, Tabitha!"

"Whoa! Wait a minute, Mona. I'm not a publicist."

"Maybe not, but you're beautiful and smart and good with people. Besides, I've done all the preparations. This is the easy part. And you'll get to travel free on my company credit card."

"But, Mona—"

"This is a big opportunity for me, Tabitha. It's my chance to prove myself to New York publishers. Please say you'll do it."

"I—I guess I could, but what if I mess up?"

"You won't. Pack your business suits and whatever else you need and come see me here at the hospital. I'll give you the keys to my office so you can get the necessary papers. Don't worry, it'll be fun!"

Fun? The jury was still out on that, but it would be an experience. Besides, she had nothing holding her in Fort Worth.... "Okay. By the way, who is this person?"

"I talked to you about him. Dr. Alex Myerson. He's the psychologist you wrote up a training plan for at the club."

"Did Dr. Myerson follow my plan?"

"Absolutely, and he looks wonderful. He'll easily impress all the interviewers."

An all-expense-paid trip *and* a handsome guy? Tabitha smiled to herself. The summer was looking better already.

The next morning, dressed in her best suit, a red one that accentuated her blond hair, Tabitha arrived at the airport. In one hand she carried Mona's briefcase, crammed with every detail of the tour. In the other, she held a publicity photo of her client, so she could recognize him.

She found him sitting in the waiting area by their gate. Mona was right. Alex Myerson was handsome, with light-brown hair, hazel eyes and a perfect body, thanks to her workout plan.

"Good morning, Dr. Myerson," she said, smiling.

He looked up, letting his gaze cover her from head to toe. Then he muttered, "Not interested."

Startled by his response, Tabitha stammered, "I—I beg your pardon?"

"I don't know where you got my name, but I don't want to make any new friends today. I'm leaving town."

"Of course you are. With me." Why was he acting so strangely?

He stood and looked down at her. "Lady, I'm not going anywhere with you. I don't even know you."

"Didn't Mona tell you?" Tabitha couldn't believe Mona would forget that important part.

"Tell me what?"

"About the accident...and the tour."

"The last I heard from Mona was a few days ago when she gave me my ticket for the first flight."

Tabitha sat down hurriedly, not sure her knees could hold her. She pulled out Mona's cell phone and dialed her number at the hospital. "Mona, you forgot to tell Dr. Myerson!"

"Oh, Tabitha, I took pain pills last night and fell asleep before I could call!"

"He's here with me now, Mona. Can you explain to him what happened?"

She handed the phone to Dr. Myerson, who didn't look as though he wanted to talk to Mona.

"Hello?" he snapped as he took the phone.

Tabitha sat wondering if this tour was to be the shortest one on record, ending only minutes after it had begun.

"We will now begin boarding Flight one-nine-eight to San Francisco. All first-class passengers are invited to board now, please."

Tabitha stood and reached out for the phone. "I'm sorry, but we have to board now."

He handed her the phone, not looking any happier than he'd been before he learned of Mona's accident.

He folded the newspaper he'd been reading, stuck it under his arm, picked up his laptop and headed for the gate without saying a word.

Okay, so the good doctor had major attitude.

Tabitha picked up her briefcase and followed him onto the plane. He might think he could ignore her, but he had another think coming.

Alex knew he'd been rude. But the events of the morning were a complete disaster. He hadn't wanted to go on this tour in the first place, despite his publisher's insistence.

After he'd met Mona, he'd finally agreed. A pleasant woman approaching fifty, Mona didn't flirt or try to get too personal. In fact, she'd assured him she was only there to make his trip run smoothly.

Since this was his first foray into a real social situation since his beloved Jenny had died a year ago, Alex had been worried. Mona had put him at ease. He'd even stopped dreading the tour.

Until this morning.

When he discovered the sexy blonde in the sleek designer suit was replacing the comfortable Mona, he couldn't speak, couldn't look at her. He was going to spend six weeks with this woman? He wouldn't survive. How could he get out of the tour?

His options faded as the plane pushed away from the gate. Panic built in him.

The blue-eyed blonde leaned over. "Are you a bad flier, Dr. Myerson?" There was sympathy in her voice, which made him even angrier.

"No, I'm not!"

Rather than retaliate, which he deserved, she put her briefcase on her lap and opened it, drawing out a folder on San Francisco. She ignored him as she read.

Finally he muttered in a low voice, "I'm sorry, Miss Tyler, but I'm not sure this tour should continue. Mona— I was comfortable with her."

"I'm not surprised. Mona is a comfortable friend, isn't she? But if she loses this tour, she's afraid she might lose her business. That's why I'm here. I just finished teaching and am now on summer vacation. This tour was not in my plans, but I'll do my best to make it successful, if you'll give me a chance."

That was the longest speech of their short acquaintance.

Alex drew a deep breath. "I'm used to being left alone, but I still shouldn't have been such a bear this morning. You took me by surprise."

"I'm sure it was a shock. I'll try to limit our interaction." Her voice was cool, unemotional. "Mona received some likely questions for your first interview this afternoon. Do you want to read them, or shall I read them to you and let you practice your response?"

"I'll read them," he said, returning to his grouchy demeanor.

She handed him the paper without comment.

It only took thirty seconds for him to erupt again. "I can't answer these questions!" he exclaimed and practically threw the paper in her face.

Catching the paper, she read the questions.

He turned his head toward the window, not wanting her to see how upset he was.

"Dr. Myerson, what is your book about?"

He turned around to stare at her. "You're my publicist and you don't even know what it's about?" he thundered.

The stewardess popped up beside their seats. "Is everything all right?"

"Yes, we're fine," Tabitha said calmly. "But it would be nice to have something to drink."

"Of course. What can I get you?"

"I'd like a diet cola. Dr. Myerson, would you care for something to drink?"

"Yes, thank you. I'd like an orange juice," he said.

They sat silently for several minutes, then his companion reminded him, "I only agreed to go yesterday afternoon, Dr. Myerson. Certainly I'll read your book as soon as possible. I asked about your book because I'm not sure why these questions are unacceptable."

"Those are personal questions. I don't talk about my personal life!" He wanted to be sure she understood where he was drawing the line.

"And why does your book draw these kinds of questions?"

"It's—it's about my marriage."

"And you think your wife will object?"

He hesitated. Then he said firmly, "Yes."

Bending over, he took a book out of his laptop bag. "Here. You can read on the plane."

"Thank you. While I'm reading, you need to think of alternative questions that you think will best sell your book. We can't leave an interviewer with nothing to say."

He glowered at her, but her statement made sense. Reluctantly, he pulled out pen and paper and put down his tray. "Fine. I'll write some questions."

Tabitha feared Dr. Myerson's book would be as difficult to read as he was to talk to. How Mona had thought it would do him good to be interviewed, Tabitha didn't know.

She settled back in her seat and opened *Making the Most of Life*. Based on what she'd seen of him, she didn't think the title was appropriate for this man.

Before she started reading, she checked the dust jacket for his bio. There was no picture and only a short blurb, saying Dr. Alex Myerson had been educated in the east, where he was awarded a Ph.D. He'd had a successful New York City practice before moving to Texas. A few words, Tabitha thought, just like the man himself.

Opening to page one, she began to read. It was hours later when she finally closed the book, her emotions stirred. The book was a personal exploration of the marital relationship between Dr. Myerson and his wife, Jenny.

"You're a fast reader," he said, snapping her from her thoughts.

"Yes, I enjoy reading." She paused, trying to think how to pose the next question she had to ask. "Your book is wonderful. It's also very personal. Don't you understand why the interviewer might want to ask personal questions?"

His jaw squared and he stared straight ahead. "No personal questions."

"May I see the questions you've devised?"

He handed over a piece of paper. Tabitha slowly read what he'd written. They demonstrated the man's intelligence, if the book hadn't already done so. What fascinated her was the difference between the man beside her and the man who'd written the book. The author had had such warmth, such caring. He and his wife shared such a beautiful existence, all because his wife had taught him to enjoy life.

Though wealthy, Alex was the product of a miserable marriage, which had provided him with a miserable childhood. He had studied psychology to learn to deal with his own problems in life. And because of his parents' debacle, he'd determined never to marry.

Until he met Jenny.

"Your wife sounds like a wonderful person, Dr. Myerson. Are you sure she would object to *all* the questions about your marriage?"

"Yes, all of them."

Tabitha sighed. Mona hadn't warned her how difficult the man could be. She looked at his questions again. Taking out a pen, she made some changes that would personalize the questions a little more, but would not totally focus on the man's own life.

Then she handed the paper back to him. "Can you live with these?"

He took the paper back and reread the questions with her changes.

Tabitha was patient, relaxing in her seat and sipping what was left of her soda.

"You're not a dumb blonde, are you?"

"Shall I take that as a compliment, Dr. Myerson?"

She was working awfully hard to satisfy this man. Mona really owed her!

"Yes. I misjudged you, Miss Tyler. Yes, I can accept these questions, as long as you explain to the interviewer that I do not want to talk about my personal life."

"I'll do the best I can, Dr. Myerson, but I can't control these people."

"Did you have that problem when you did your tour?"

"Absolutely. All the men wanted to discuss my sex life. All the women wanted to know what I ate, implying that I lived on watercress sandwiches."

His chuckle seemed to surprise both of them, as if he hadn't laughed in a long time. "I can see their point," he finally said.

Gently, she said, "After reading your book, I can understand why they would want to ask you about your marriage."

He stared out the window, saying nothing.

Suddenly, a horrible thought struck her. "Oh, no! You haven't just gone through a divorce, have you? Because someone will find out and it will destroy the tour. Tell me now if that's the case."

Glaring at her, he shook his head. "That's not the case!"

She breathed a sigh of relief. "Good. Then we'll be all right, as long as you don't lose your cool. If they ask you something personal, just steer it toward generalizations. I'm sure your wife won't mind that."

At that moment the flight attendant interrupted to serve them lunch. Tabitha abandoned any pretense of conversation. It was hard enough when she was concentrating on it, but she wanted to enjoy her meal.

Not surprisingly, Myerson remained silent too. She took the opportunity to sneak a glance at her companion and study him surreptitiously. His jawline looked as if it was chiseled from granite, hard and sharp-edged, and the firm set of his mouth added to his imposing look.

Still, she knew he had a sensitive side, though it had yet to show itself. Jenny, his wife, no doubt had brought it out in him. Was that it? she wondered suddenly. His moodiness was a result of missing her? She could help that.

"Dr. Myerson, if you want your wife to join you for part of the trip, I can arrange flights for her. Just let me know."

"That won't be necessary."

"Really, Mona wants you to be happy, and after reading your book, it's easy to see how close you are to Jenny, so I'd be glad to—"

"No, she can't join me!" His voice was harsh again.

"Why not?"

She thought he wasn't going to answer her question. But he finally did. "Because she's dead, Miss Tyler. Now will you leave it alone?"

Mona certainly hadn't told her that. "I'm sorry. When—"

"A year ago today."

Alex hadn't intended to tell anyone of Jenny's death. He had kept his mourning to himself. Jenny hadn't had family, and his didn't care, so he'd tried to appear as if nothing had happened.

He'd begun the book a couple of months before Jenny had failed to return from the store one evening. That night several police officers had knocked on his door, telling him a truck driver had fallen asleep at the wheel and killed three people. Jenny was one of the victims. He'd finished the book as a posthumous tribute to his wonderful wife.

He was sure, however, that he couldn't talk about Jenny during the interviews. He'd lose emotional control. And he didn't want people to buy his book because they pitied him.

Staring out the window the rest of the flight, he said nothing to the young woman beside him. She was even more beautiful than Jenny, and unlike his wife she had the gift of life. He hoped she appreciated it.

When they finally left the plane, she offered to carry his laptop case for him, in addition to her own briefcase. Did she think grief had incapacitated him?

That thought angered him even more.

He didn't want to think about his grief.

"No thanks," he ground out. "I'm fine."

"Very well." She went down the aisle ahead of him. When they reached the walkway, she said, "I'll meet you at the baggage claim."

"Where are you going?" he demanded.

"I'm going to the ladies' room. Did you want to accompany me?"

"No," he growled. He'd deserved that response, he supposed. But she sure wasn't Mona.

He already had his bags off the baggage carousel when she found him.

"Show me your bags and I'll get them for you," he said. It was his way of apologizing again.

"No need. I have a porter with me," she assured him. "Oscar, these are Dr. Myerson's bags, if you want to put them on the trolley." A minute later she pointed to the carousel. "Oh, there they are. Those two tan bags. Thank you, Oscar," she added as the porter snagged her bags. "Now we need a taxi, and we'll be on our way."

"Right this way, Miss Tyler," Oscar said.

Alex frowned. She'd certainly gotten friendly with the man in a short period of time.

When they got in the taxi, after tipping Oscar, she instructed the driver on their destination. Then she turned to Alex.

"I thought we'd check into the hotel and have an hour or two to relax before we go to the interview. After that, you have the signing. We won't get dinner until late, so I'll order a snack for you. If you want to look at the room-service menu, you can tell me what you'd like."

He nodded. He knew Mona had said she'd make his life easy, but somehow it bothered him that this woman was so in control over him.

Once they arrived in downtown San Francisco they entered a beautiful hotel, whose reception area looked out at an incredible garden. Miss Tyler came to a halt, gasping at the riotous color of the flowers. "How lovely!"

"Yes," he said without thinking, "Jenny would've loved it." Realizing what he said, he stepped back and frowned at his companion. "I mean, yes, it's beautiful."

She gave him a sympathetic smile and continued on her way to the reception desk.

It didn't take much perception to notice all the men staring at his guide. Tabitha Tyler certainly took the attention in stride.

"Doesn't it bother you that all the men are staring at you?" he demanded.

"No, I'm quite used to it."

She must've seen the withdrawal from such arrogance in his eyes.

Laughing, she said, "Because I'm one of three. My sisters and I are triplets, Dr. Myerson. People have been staring at us since we were born."

"Triplets? Do they look just like you?" he asked in astonishment. He couldn't imagine three of Tabitha Tyler.

"Yes, except that we each wear our hair differently. Mine's the longest." She found the shortest line for registration and stood patiently waiting. "The hotel seems awfully crowded."

"Probably a convention," he said absent-mindedly, still picturing three of her.

"Don't worry. I called and confirmed our reservations yesterday."

When their turn came, Tabitha greeted the young man with a smile and gave their names.

"Welcome, Miss Tyler." The clerk, who'd maintained his cheerfulness despite the swarm of incoming guests, typed on his keypad, then gave her a white-toothed smile. "We assumed, since you're traveling together, you would prefer connecting rooms."

Chapter Two

Alex stared at the man, not believing what he'd heard. Their rooms were going to be connected by a door? That simply wouldn't do.

Beside him he heard Miss Tyler calmly say, "Is that all you have to offer?"

"Yes, ma'am, I'm afraid we're totally booked," the clerk returned. "But you'll have easy access to your client this way. You know, we went to a lot of trouble to save these two rooms for you."

"Very well," the woman agreed.

Agreed? Was she kidding him?

Alex grabbed her sleeve. Through clenched teeth he whispered, "I won't stand for this! I want a room alone."

"But there are no other accommodations, Dr. Myerson. It's all right. I won't be barging in on you. All you have to do is close the door to my room and lock it."

She signed the charge card receipt and received the two keycards the clerk handed her. In turn, she handed one of them to Alex. Then she gave the bellhop a tip and her room number. "Ready to go up?"

"Yeah." He glowered at her as he spoke.

Keeping a smile on her face, she moved to the elevators as if everything was hunky-dory. Which only irritated him more.

"This isn't going to work," he muttered under his breath in the elevator.

"It will be fine, Dr. Myerson," she insisted, whispering also.

The elderly woman in front of them turned to face them. "Young man, if you're having second thoughts, you shouldn't go in that room with her. After all, you're a married man, aren't you?"

Suddenly Miss Tyler wasn't as calm as she had been. Her voice held an icy tone that frosted the elevator car. "We don't need your advice, ma'am."

"When he's already doubting the wisdom of spending the night with you, I should think you'd be too proud to go ahead with your plans."

Luckily the elevator stopped then on their floor. Without even a glance to the older woman, Miss Tyler took Alex by the arm and started out.

As soon as the door closed behind him, Alex wrenched his arm from her hold. "I don't like to be touched!"

She stared at him, opening her mouth as if she was going to say something impetuously. Then she closed it and went down the corridor to their rooms. When he joined her, she said coolly, "I'll keep that in mind, Dr. Myerson."

She slipped the keycard in the lock and opened his door, standing back for him to precede her into the room. The suite had a small living room with floor-to-ceiling windows that presented a glorious view of Fisherman's Wharf and the Golden Gate Bridge.

"Oh, my! I've always heard about the beauty of San Francisco, but this is even more beautiful than I imagined."

She swung around, a broad smile on her face, as if she expected him to join her at the window.

He ignored her. He wasn't going to talk about the view, or how much she reminded him of Jenny. Until he was alone, he couldn't regain his composure.

After a sigh, she walked over to the door and opened it to another door. "Here's the connecting door, Dr. Myerson." She checked her watch. "You have two and a half hours before you have to appear for the interview. When you're ready for a snack, knock and let me know."

After he nodded, she walked out to the hall, closing the door behind her.

A pristine king-size bed, drew him and he flopped down on his back. Damn! One day on tour and the woman was driving him crazy!

Not that he was attracted to her. Of course not! But sometimes she reminded him of Jenny. Those feelings were painful. When she'd touched him, he'd wanted to shake off her hold at once. There was some kind of odd chemistry between them, he had to admit. One he intended to avoid from now on.

A knock on the door grabbed his attention. He was relieved to realize it was the hall door. He opened it and found the bellhop there with the luggage.

"Come in," he said, swinging the door wide. Then he knocked on the connecting door. When Miss Tyler opened the door, he nodded in the direction of the bellhop, who entered her room.

Alex closed the door and lay back down on the bed, but he had to get up only a couple of minutes later when someone knocked on the connecting door. He assumed the bellhop had forgotten something. When he swung the door open, he found Tabitha Tyler standing there.

"Yes?"

"If you won't need me for an hour, I'm going up to the gym to work out. It relieves my tension."

If she'd had any tension, she'd hidden it, except for her reaction to the busybody in the elevator. But her solution to relieving taut muscles appealed to him. Since Mona had put him on a fitness regimen, he'd learned the value of exercise. "Mind if I go up with you? I'd like to work out, too."

Though she looked surprised, she nodded. "Of course. I'll be ready in about ten minutes. Just knock on the door when you're ready."

He nodded and shut the door again. Then he hurriedly opened his bag to take out some workout clothes. He'd be able to handle the interview better after working out.

When he knocked on the door and she opened it, he realized his mistake. Tabitha Tyler in workout clothes was quite different from the sleek young woman in a designer suit. That suit had hinted at curves in all the right places. Her leotard and tights left nothing to the imagination.

He wasn't sure exercise would reduce his tension if Tabitha Tyler was in his line of vision.

Tabitha had taken one of her videos with her to the gym. After a quick warm-up, she put her tape in the video player and began her exercise program for aerobic training. Before she knew it, she'd drawn three or four other women who were following the video. When she finished the forty-five-minute tape, the ladies asked where they could get a copy.

Tabitha gave them the Web site where they could order the tape. Then she looked for her charge. Earlier he'd been working out on some of the machines, but now she spotted him jogging on the indoor track.

"Dr. Myerson?" she called and jogged onto the track to catch up with him.

"Yes?" he said, not stopping.

"I've finished working out. Are you ready to go back to the room?"

"No, I'll be up in a minute."

"What kind of snack would you like? I'll order it before I get in the shower."

"Surprise me," he said abruptly.

She stopped jogging and stepped off the track, her hands on her hips. "Okay!" she muttered. The man was determined to be difficult. Fine, she'd please herself.

Once she'd reached her room, she checked the menu. They had a sampler tray of various hors d'oeuvres.

Surely something on the tray would tempt Dr. Myerson, assuming he ever allowed anything to tempt him!

They promised delivery in fifteen to twenty minutes, so she hurried into the bathroom for a quick shower. With time to spare she was dressed in a blouse and tailored slacks, her hair already dried and curled with a curling iron. She'd learned to dress quickly when she was in college and constantly overslept.

The waiter delivered the sampler tray and several sodas. As soon as he'd left the room, she knocked on the connecting door. There was no answer.

"Great!" She didn't know if he was there and in the shower, hadn't come back yet or wouldn't answer because he wanted to be left alone.

She walked over to the windows to stare at the city and bay. It was impressive.

Surprisingly, there was a knock on the connecting door. She spun around and hurried to it.

"Dr. Myerson, come in. Our snack is here."

He too was already dressed, in a dark suit with a blue shirt. "I was dressing when you knocked on the door. Sorry to keep you waiting," he said.

There was no smile, but at least he had developed some good manners. "No problem. I ordered a sampler tray to be sure I found something you'd like."

"Thank you." He helped himself to a drink and poured a diet soda for her.

She thanked him and sat on the sofa opposite his matching chair. They ate in complete silence. Finally, when Tabitha could stand it no longer, she asked, "Are you nervous about the interview, Dr. Myerson?"

"No."

"Have you been to San Francisco before?"

"Yes."

Tabitha sighed. Talk about hard work!

"When were you here?" she persisted, hoping to find some topic to talk about.

"I was here four years ago on my honeymoon." This time his voice was steely, daring her to continue.

"I see. I didn't realize how difficult this trip would be for you. We'll need to leave in about half an hour. If you'll excuse me, I need to do a little work before we go."

She stood and moved to the table where she took out her files and thought about calling Mona. This tour was a disaster before his first interview!

Alex knew he'd been difficult. After she moved to the table, he stood and walked to the window, his hands in his pockets.

He needed to get himself under control. His behavior wasn't going to bring Jenny back. Had he really thought if he didn't share her death with anyone, it would be easier? If that was true, then he was worse than his patients.

If he kept his cool and did good interviews, more people might buy his book and understand about Jenny. He wanted people to know his wife, to appreciate the kind of person she was.

He didn't want them to know how devastated he was.

After a quick glance at Miss Tyler, he went to his room. He needed to make sure his mind was organized.

And he needed to stop making Miss Tyler the enemy.

She'd done as Mona promised, made his trip more comfortable. And he hadn't been very appreciative. For Jenny's sake, he owed her an apology. But it was difficult. She was extremely attractive and he felt some kind of reaction when they touched. And when he watched her exercising.

So he didn't want to touch her. But he could be more cooperative. He could use good manners, at least…couldn't he?

Alex sat on the edge of his bed. He'd hidden away from the world since Jenny died. The only contact he'd had was with his publisher and then Mona, and a few patients he still had.

It wasn't healthy. He knew that, but he'd shoved aside what he'd learned in his studies, as if none of it applied to him. But he'd been wrong.

One day spent in the real world was an awakening he didn't welcome. But if he continued on the tour, he had no choice.

He had to come to terms with the reality that Jenny would never come back.

With her makeup applied and her jacket on, Tabitha drew a deep breath, prepared to face the dragon in the next room. Every time he spoke, she saw an imaginary flame come out of his mouth, warning her not to approach him. If he continued to behave in such a manner, she didn't think his interviews would go well.

When she knocked on the door, Dr. Myerson opened it at once.

"We need to leave now to be sure we get there a little early." She smiled, even though she expected no smile in return. Turning on her heel, she led the way to the door.

When they reached the elevator, she kept her distance, remembering his remark that he didn't like to be touched. It still amazed her that he could've written that inspired book. She intended to reread it after the tour.

When they got in the taxi, she looked at her notes once more. "The interviewer is Helen Wilson, a life-styles reporter. I'll give her the questions we worked on and talk to her about the limitations you want her to follow."

"Thank you. I want to apologize for my behavior, Tabitha. And I hope you'll call me Alex. It's...unfriendly to remain so formal."

Tabitha turned to her companion. He was staring straight ahead, his features devoid of emotion. She wondered if she'd imagined his words. "That will be fine...Alex."

"I appreciate the patience you've shown."

He was like a ventriloquist, speaking without moving his lips. She blinked several times. Then she said, "Perhaps you'll tell my sisters that. Though I doubt they'd believe you."

That response actually made him turn his head to look at her. "Your sisters? The other two of the triplets?"

"Yes. I'm the most impatient of the three of us."

"I've thought about doing a study of multiple births," he said slowly. "But most people don't like to be studied."

Tabitha smiled. "That's because they've been stared at too often. We enjoy each other's company, but when the three of us appear together, we have to deal with a lot of surprise and questions."

"Do you resent it?" he asked, showing interest for the first time.

"No, not exactly. We just get tired of feeling like circus freaks."

"Did your mother dress you alike?"

"When we were little, she did. But when we got old enough to make our own decisions, that ended. Our closet was a free-for-all." She smiled as she reminisced.

"I was an only child," he said, frowning.

"I'm sorry. That must've been—" She caught herself and took a different approach. "Some people like that, though, because they're the center of their parents' attention."

He didn't respond.

She didn't know why he changed back to his silent mode, but she regretted whatever she'd said that offended him. The taxi pulled to a stop and she mentally promised she'd apologize later.

Once they were in the television studio, she met Helen Wilson, an effervescent woman who swept everyone along in her wake.

"I'm so excited to meet Dr. Myerson. His book is so wonderful. It's like falling in love all over again when I read it."

"That's a wonderful way to describe it, Helen," Tabitha said, feeling better about the interview. "However, Dr. Myerson wants to focus on the applications people can find in his book rather than on the—the personal aspects."

"Well, of course, he wants his readers to benefit from

his wisdom. By the way, did his wife accompany him? I'd love to meet her."

Tabitha carefully controlled her expression. "No, she didn't."

"That's too bad, but Dr. Myerson will be quite enough for our audience. I'm sure he's charming."

Tabitha smiled, not showing her doubts about his charm. "Yes, of course. Shall I introduce you now?"

Mentally crossing her fingers, Tabitha led Helen over to Dr. Myerson. Alex, she reminded herself.

"Alex, allow me to present Helen Wilson, your interviewer. She loved your book." She hoped her bright smile might induce him to warm up a little.

To her surprise, he took Helen's hand and smiled at her, as if he were delighted to be there. Tabitha blinked, wondering if she was seeing clearly.

"I'm pleased to meet you, Helen. I love your beautiful city."

"I know. I feel privileged to live here. Have you visited us before?"

"Yes, but it's been awhile."

"We're glad you came back." Helen tucked her arm into Alex's and drew him with her to the set in front of the television cameras.

Tabitha had sucked in a sharp breath when Helen reached out and touched Alex, afraid his reaction would be unfriendly. Instead, one would think he escorted women around the town all the time.

Taking a seat behind the cameras so she could watch the interview, Tabitha prayed Helen kept the discussion away from Alex's wife. In spite of the wonderful behavior he'd shown the interviewer, she wasn't sure it would continue.

Half an hour later, she stood and applauded as did everyone on the set. Helen had asked the right kind of questions, and Alex had been more relaxed, more charming, than Tabitha had ever seen him. She walked over to shake Helen's hand and commend her for the wonderful job she'd done.

When she turned to Alex, intending to repeat her compliments, he leaned close to her and growled, "Get me the hell out of here!"

Again, his facial features didn't match his words. She was beginning to think she *was* dealing with a ventriloquist. Facing Helen again, she said, "I hope you'll excuse us. We didn't have time to get anything to eat beforehand, so we're going to fit in a quick meal before the book-signing. But it was wonderful working with you this afternoon."

"Of course, I understand. Have a great book-signing, Alex."

He smiled and waved, but he was already on his way out of the studio.

"Are you all right?" Tabitha demanded when she caught up with him, fearing he might be feeling sick.

"Yes, but can we stop for coffee or something?" He continued to sprint forward.

"Yes, of course," she said, frantically trying to remember if they'd seen any coffee shops in the area. And wondering why he was acting as he was.

When they exited the studio, they saw a coffee shop down the street and walked half a block to it.

"Why don't you sit down and I'll get the coffee? Do you want decaf?"

"No, I need the caffeine," he said roughly, avoiding looking at her.

Were they returning to their earlier cold war? Tabitha hoped not. She wasn't sure she could handle six weeks of battle with Alex Myerson.

She ordered two coffees and two pieces of carrot cake. A little sugar might make it easier to get through the signing.

Carrying everything on a tray, she reached the table where Alex sat with his head in his hands. Again, she wondered what was wrong. The interview had been spectacular. She couldn't imagine what had happened that would draw the devastation she saw in his body language.

Tabitha transferred the dishes to the table. Then she returned the tray to the counter and came back to sit down in the chair across from Alex.

He hadn't raised his head. In fact, she didn't think he'd moved at all since he'd sat down. "Alex, is there anything else I can get you?"

Finally, he looked up and said no, but his gaze didn't meet hers.

She shoved his coffee and cake closer to him. "Do you like carrot cake? It's one of my favorites."

Instead of answering, he picked up the cup and took a sip of coffee.

Tabitha gave it another try. "The interview went really well. I think it—"

Alex raised his gaze to meet hers, fire in his eyes. With outrage in his voice, he shouted, "Stop!"

Chapter Three

Tabitha stared at him. "What? What did I do?"

"I thought I was doing the right thing, but it was a sell-out!"

She could see anger in his eyes. The man was in pain. Without thinking, she reached out to touch his hand, forgetting that he'd said he didn't want to be touched.

He withdrew at once.

"Sorry." Tabitha pulled her hand back, but she couldn't let him sit there without trying to find out what his problem was. "Alex, please tell me what's wrong. I can't help you until you do."

"I had promised myself I'd stop being difficult. I did the interview, trying to sell books. Then I realized I'd betrayed Jenny! I was *using* her to sell books!"

Tabitha drew a deep breath. There was no doubt that his anguish was real. After reading the book herself, she knew he and his wife had shared a deep love. Slowly, she said, "I thought you wanted people to know Jenny, to appreciate her."

"I did! But—but the longer the interview went on, the more I—" He buried his head in his hands again.

"Alex, the reason you wrote the book is because you thought you had learned something that would help other people, right?"

He nodded.

"Well, if they don't read the book, they won't understand what you have to say. You didn't betray Jenny. She would want your book to be a success even if she didn't believe in what you wrote. But she did. It's obvious in the book. She believed in you and loved you."

"But—"

"Am I right?"

"Yes."

"Then you did exactly what Jenny would want you to do."

"I didn't think of it like that." Alex straightened his shoulders. "Maybe you're right."

"I assure you I am. Now, eat your cake and drink the coffee." She did the same, but she kept an eye on Alex. It appeared to her he'd panicked because he hadn't discussed his wife or their marriage with anyone before. Today, he'd been forced to open up a little. And it bothered him.

Slowly, he calmed down, thanks to the coffee and cake. She hoped he'd be in shape for his signing, which would start in less than an hour.

When he'd almost finished, she said, "How would

you feel about returning to the station to tell Helen the truth?"

His head snapped up. "Why would I do that?"

"People are going to find out that Jenny is dead. When Helen finds out, she's going to feel that you lied to her. She did a really good job with the interview. If you take her into your confidence, she won't be angry. She'll be flattered."

She thought he wasn't going to answer. He merely sat there, staring over his coffee cup at an unseen spot on the wall behind her.

Finally, he said, "I suppose you're right."

He stood, looking down at her. "You're going with me, aren't you?"

"Of course." She rose at once, but cast a longing look at the rest of her carrot cake.

They walked the half block back to the studio. Just as they reached it, Helen Wilson walked out.

"Helen," Alex called.

She turned around and came over to them. "Alex, I thought you left long ago."

"We did, but I—"

"I thought you were going to get something to eat."

Alex frowned at Tabitha, as if suddenly debating the wisdom of her advice. "We were, but we decided to wait until after the signing."

"I see. Then what—"

"I need to tell you something." Alex was concentrating on what he had to say so much, Tabitha didn't think he even realized he'd interrupted Helen.

"Yes, of course," she said, moving closer.

"My wife is dead."

"Dead? Jenny is dead?" Helen responded, sounding a bit alarmed.

Tabitha, sensing the woman's train of thought, stepped forward when it appeared Alex wasn't going to explain. "Jenny died a year ago, in a car accident." She could see the alarm on Helen's face slowly dissipate, to be replaced by confusion. Tabitha continued, "Alex had started the book while she was alive and finished it as a tribute to their love. He was afraid if he let people know she'd died, they might buy the book out of sympathy. And he also has difficulty talking about Jenny."

"Well, of course, I understand."

"You were so kind today, Alex didn't want you to think he'd lied to you."

"Oh, Alex," Helen cooed, moving closer and taking his hand in hers. "You are so wonderful. Let me buy you dinner after the book-signing. We have so much in common. I'm a widow, you know." She leaned forward and kissed his cheek. "I have to run now, but I'll see you at the bookstore."

Before either Alex or Tabitha could speak, she was gone.

Alex turned slowly around to stare at her. "That's the last time I'll take your advice!" he exclaimed.

"I didn't expect her to—to immediately see you as a potential mate," Tabitha protested.

"What? A potential mate? She's at least ten years older than me!"

"Age doesn't matter much these days."

"It matters to me. Besides, I'm not looking for a woman."

"I guess you could develop a headache when she arrives," Tabitha suggested with a grin.

"I have a better idea," Alex said, glaring at her.

"Uh-oh, I don't think I'm going to like it."

"Probably not. But you're going with us."

"No! I wasn't invited!"

"I assumed she meant both of us." He smiled at her, and then he pointed out that they needed to get to the bookstore.

Tabitha checked her watch and realized they only had twenty minutes before they were supposed to be there. The bookstore people had asked them to arrive half an hour early.

Once they were in the taxi, she tried again. "Alex, I can't go with you. She didn't invite me!"

"Either you go with me or I tell Helen I refuse to go with her, which will upset her."

"It's going to upset her even more if I play chaperone."

"What would Mona do?"

"That's unfair, Alex!"

"I think Mona would protect me from a man-hungry woman."

"I think you're a fraud, Alex Myerson. You handled Helen just fine in the interview. You can survive dinner with her." She held her breath, hoping her challenge would convince him.

He looked at her and shook his head, a grin slowly forming on his lips. A very charming grin. No wonder Helen was after him.

"Fine! I'll go with you. But you owe me, Alex. No more being difficult."

"Agreed." Then he drew a deep breath. "I really appreciate your getting me through this evening. I won't fall apart again."

"Just doing my job," she said with a smile. "Though I'll admit I was thinking about resigning earlier."

He suddenly turned serious. "I'm glad you didn't."

When the taxi pulled up in front of the bookstore, Tabitha hurriedly paid the driver. Alex got out of the taxi and stood there, holding the door open for her. She scooted across the seat and stepped out.

"We're right on time," she announced. Taking his arm, she started toward the store. Then she remembered that he didn't want to be touched and jerked her arm back. "Sorry."

But Alex didn't say anything.

In the store, Tabitha quickly found the manager and introduced herself as Mona's replacement. "And this is my client, Dr. Alex Myerson."

Alex shook the man's hand.

"Welcome, Dr. Myerson. Your books are set up over here, near the door. We have a pitcher of water and glasses and black-inked pens, as you requested. Is there anything else we can get you?"

"No, I don't think so. However, this is my first signing, so if I think of anything, may I have a rain check?"

"Absolutely. By the way, I saw your interview on the afternoon show. It was wonderful. We've been getting phone calls ever since the interview."

"Really?" Alex asked, his eyebrows going up in surprise.

"Absolutely. We're expecting a wonderful turnout."

Alex looked at Tabitha, and she smiled encouragingly. She wasn't sure he was happy about a large crowd.

Fifteen minutes before the signing was to begin, the store began to fill with women who surrounded the table where Alex's books were piled high. Tabitha and Alex were sitting in the coffee shop that was part of the bookstore.

"You feel like starting early?" she asked. "You already have a crowd."

"Not really. But I guess I could."

She went to the manager, offering to start the signing early.

"That would be wonderful. We'll get them in line if Dr. Myerson will do that."

Tabitha waved Alex on. When he walked toward her, several women saw him and screamed out his name. Alex came to an abrupt halt, staring at the women in shock.

Tabitha crossed to his side. "Come on, I'll protect you," she whispered.

Careful not to touch him, and not to let any of the crowd touch him either, she ushered him to the table.

Once he was ensconced behind the wooden barrier, Alex seemed to relax. He greeted each woman and signed a book to her. There were even a few men in the line. He spent more time with them.

The signing was supposed to last an hour and a half, but Alex continued to sign as long as there were people there. Then the bookstore people asked him to sign a few extra copies for them to put on the shelves with an autographed-copy sticker on them.

Tabitha had seen Helen come in a while ago and she saw her check her watch every five minutes, seeming to grow impatient.

Tabitha grinned. Helen thought she was unhappy now, but wait till she heard her evening would include Tabitha as a chaperone.

Alex saw Helen as soon as she came in the bookstore. He could hardly miss her since she waved to him, calling his name while he was signing a book. Until then, he'd had his doubts about Tabitha's interpretation of Helen's intent.

Dressed in a silver lamé dress that dropped low in front, ensuring that he got a good glimpse of her décolletage, Helen was hunting. No doubt about it. Now he was grateful he'd convinced Tabitha to come along with them. After all it had been awhile since he'd dealt with an aggressive female.

In fact, it was only since he'd begun to work out, at Mona's behest, that he'd had the form that attracted women. Jenny had loved him as he'd been.

He looked to be sure Tabitha saw Helen. Of course, her appearance wouldn't surprise Tabitha. But he thought the dress Helen was wearing would be a lot more interesting on Tabitha's svelte body. Thanks to her exercise regimen, she didn't have an ounce of fat on her.

When he'd finally finished the signing, Helen appeared at his side.

"I didn't think you'd ever get done." A satisfied smile lit up her made-up eyes.

"Thanks to your wonderful interview, we had a crowd waiting," he told her with a grin. "To show our appreciation, Tabitha is going to host our little dinner party tonight. The three of us have a lot to celebrate." He hadn't mentioned that to Tabitha, but he'd promise to reimburse her if she'd go along.

"Oh, but I—"

"Here's Tabitha now. Tabitha, I was just telling Helen we owe this wonderful signing to her, so you wanted to take both of us out to dinner to celebrate." He stared intently at her, hoping to quell any resistance.

"He's absolutely right," Tabitha assured Helen, relieving Alex's concerns at once. "I made reservations for us at a lovely restaurant in our hotel." She looked at her watch. "We're going to have to dash. I'll go flag down a taxi."

Tabitha scooted off before Alex could stop her. He didn't want to spend any time alone with Helen. Of course, Helen immediately began to complain, but Alex merely led her to the door, stopping only to thank the store manager, who was ecstatic.

Outside, he discovered Tabitha had already gotten a taxi and was holding open the door to the back seat. Alex assumed she'd follow them into the back, but she shut the door and got in the front seat with the driver.

Helen snuggled up to him and Alex had the vision of her leaving makeup tracks on his suit. He sought desperately for a subject of conversation, fearing she'd try to kiss him if he didn't divert her.

"Uh, Helen, how long have you been a widow?"

"Several years. It's hard to get back out there, isn't it?"

"Yeah. What did your husband do for a living?"

"Not much. I was always the breadwinner. But I managed."

He was getting no help from Tabitha, who was chatting with the driver as if she had no interest in the backseat conversation.

"I love the cable cars," he said as one passed by. "They're so interesting."

"Yes, they're one of the perks of living in San Francisco. That and the view. Everywhere you look, you see the blue of the water. It's magnificent. If you lived here, Alex, you'd be inspired to write all the time."

"I think I'd be inspired to play hooky," he returned.

"Oh, Alex, I'm sure—"

She never finished her remark, because as soon as the taxi pulled up in front of their hotel, Alex opened his door and got out. He breathed a sigh of relief…until Helen, now beside him, shot him a fluttery smile telling him he hadn't discouraged her.

Tabitha came to his aid.

"Have you eaten at this restaurant before, Helen?" she asked, trying to distract the woman's attentions.

"Of course. It's part of my job to try the restaurants."

Her tone was rather standoffish toward Tabitha, whom she clearly hadn't forgiven for horning in on their date. But Alex smiled in gratitude.

"What do you recommend?" Tabitha asked her.

"They do fish well. Their crème brûlée is fabulous."

Then she shrugged her shoulders. "Actually, anything they serve is wonderful."

"Good. I'm glad I chose well."

When they reached the elevator to the penthouse restaurant, Alex held the door for both women. Then he moved to stand by Tabitha, leaving Helen on the other side of his chaperone.

"Do they have any decent restaurants in Fort Worth?" Helen asked, amusement in her voice.

"Why yes, we have a few." Tabitha turned to smile at Helen. "Come for a visit and we'll be glad to show you around."

"Yeah, we can take her to Joe T. Garcia's," Alex offered. "It's quite famous."

"What do they serve there?"

"It's a Mexican restaurant," Tabitha explained.

"I think my palate might be a little too sophisticated for that kind of meal. That's another of the perks of living here. Dining out is a unique experience."

"Joe T.'s is pretty unique," Alex assured Helen, a grin on his face. The lady was just a little too full of herself, he thought. "Or if you come in January, we'll take you to the Fort Worth Stock Show and Rodeo. The hot dogs are pretty good there, too."

Helen looked at him as if he'd said something shocking. Still, it was better than the melting looks she'd been sending him earlier.

"Alex is teasing, Helen. There are several nice restaurants there."

"Here, there are thousands!" she snapped.

The elevator doors opened and they entered the restaurant. All along the perimeter were walls of windows overlooking the beauty of San Francisco.

"I *know* you don't have anything that looks like this in Fort Worth, because you don't have an ocean there."

"You're right," Tabitha agreed. She stepped forward and spoke to the maître d', who showed them to a table at once.

Helen wanted to order champagne for their celebration. Tabitha agreed to do so, but she didn't care for any. Alex immediately told Helen he wouldn't drink any this late at night. Frustrated, Helen asked for a glass of the house wine.

After they ordered, Helen tried to draw Alex into intimate conversation, but it was difficult since Tabitha was sitting between them. Alex had waited until the two ladies were seated before he circled the table and took the seat by Tabitha.

All during the meal, Helen asked intimate questions in questionable good taste, and Alex responded with general answers and asked Tabitha's opinion. Finally, toward the end of their meal, Helen said, "You should've told me you and Tabitha were intimate, Alex. I wouldn't have troubled you this evening."

She stood, surprising both of them. "I'm leaving now. Thanks for the dinner, Tabitha."

When she walked out of earshot, Alex asked, "Do you think I offended her?"

"I think you tried," Tabitha said, rolling her eyes.

"I thought I was being subtle," he assured her.

"Hardly. She lasted longer than I thought she would, actually," Tabitha said. "I even felt a little sorry for her."

"Let's drown your sorrows in some crème brûlée, shall we?" Alex suggested with a grin, showing no remorse for sending Helen Wilson on her way.

"I shouldn't," Tabitha said. Then she returned Alex's grin. "But Helen did say it wasn't to be missed. And in the great city of San Francisco, we wouldn't want to pass up something really special."

"Of course not." As he signaled the waiter, he remembered something else. "By the way, I'm paying for this evening. I was going to let you pay and then reimburse you, but since Helen is gone, I can just take care of it."

"That's not necessary."

"Yes, sir?" the waiter asked when he reached the table.

"We'd both like to try the crème brûlée. It comes highly recommended."

"Oh, it *is* wonderful. You'll see," the waiter promised and withdrew after he collected their dinner plates.

"Another San Francisco enthusiast," Alex said with a sigh.

"Alex, I'll pay for the evening. Mona would want me to."

"Nope. This is my treat. As a reward for helping me scare off Helen." He made a mock shudder. "That dress was enough to scare me."

Tabitha tried to hide her laughter, but Alex grinned at her, enjoying her amusement. "It would've looked better on you."

"I don't wear lamé. It's not appropriate in Fort Worth."

"No kidding. No wonder I didn't cotton to it much."

The waiter arrived with the crème brûlée and after the first bite, they stopped and looked at each other. Alex said, "Whatever else I might say about Helen Wilson, she's got excellent taste in desserts."

"Yes, she certainly does."

"Do you go out much back home?" Alex asked abruptly.

"N-no, not much," she replied, then she immediately launched into their schedule of the next day, purposely taking the conversation from intimacy to business.

Alex waited her out. When she finally ran out of anything else to say, he countered, "You know a lot about me. I should be allowed to ask questions of you."

"I have to know about you to help you get through difficult situations. I'm not asking you to help me in any way. Therefore, you don't need to know anything about me."

Alex didn't buy her argument. "What about my desire to study multiple births? You don't mind answering questions about that, do you?"

"I—I suppose not."

"Do you and your sisters discuss your birth order? We've discovered that siblings in single births are quite aware of birth order and behave accordingly."

"Tommie is the firstborn and feels responsible for us. Is that what you mean?"

"Yes. And the youngest?"

"That's Teresa. Tommie and I both felt protective of her, but she proved she could take care of herself. In spite of having had a frightening experience."

"What happened?"

Tabitha told him about Teresa's neighbor's home having been broken into while she was next door having dinner with Teresa. The thief had stolen the spare keys Teresa had given the neighbor. Then he'd gotten into Teresa's house and destroyed almost everything in it.

"That's horrible. Where was she?"

"Luckily, she wasn't home. But the guy had Teresa's spare keys, so she couldn't stay there."

"Did she stay with you?"

"No. I didn't find out about it until the next morning. She went home with the father of her twins."

"Your sister was pregnant with twins and not married to the father?"

Though Alex had tried to keep any condemnation out of his voice, Tabitha stiffened. "Yes."

"But they're married now?"

"Yes, once he admitted that he loved her. She wasn't going to marry him just because she was pregnant. She was prepared to take care of her children alone rather than enter a loveless marriage."

"She really did prove herself to be strong."

"Yes, she did."

"Are you that strong?"

"I hope so," Tabitha said, raising her chin. "But I don't intend to be caught in that position. Teresa has always been a little naive. She was a kindergarten teacher, you know. Always looking for the good in everyone. She fell in love and believed he loved her, too."

"And he didn't?"

There was a lot of sympathy in his voice, which

Tabitha appreciated. "Actually, he did, but he'd started dating her because of his twin brother and—"

"He was a multiple birth, too?" Alex asked in surprise.

"Yes, Jim is Pete's twin brother."

"Who's Pete?"

"Tommie's husband."

"So Teresa and Tommie married twin brothers?"

She nodded. "And Teresa gave birth to twins a couple of months ago. Tommie's pregnant now, but it's only one baby."

"With all these babies do you feel a little left out?"

Tabitha sat back with a sigh. "Yes. Though I'd hoped I'd hid it well."

"Don't worry. You did. I'm just perceptive," he assured her with a grin. "Well, what about you? Are you dating any potential future husband?"

"Yes, actually, I am. I met someone a couple of months back—Derek—and...and we've been getting to know each other."

"And you like what you've seen so far?"

"Yes," she replied, a smile on her face. "Very much. I think he—"

Her remark was interrupted by the waiter, who stopped by their table. "Would you care for more coffee?"

Alex looked up in surprise, only to discover they were the last diners in the room. "No, thank you. Here's my charge card."

"Thank you, sir. I'll be right back."

"I think we've outstayed our welcome," he whispered to Tabitha in jest.

But she only nodded. In fact, she said nothing until they reached their connecting rooms. "Dr. Myerson, I owe you an apology. I should have been listening to you at dinner, not telling you all about my family and myself." She kept her head down, not looking at him.

"What? And why are you suddenly formal with me? I thought we agreed to be more casual."

"We did, but—but I shouldn't have."

"And why did you?"

Her eyes met his. "Because you kept asking questions."

"Exactly, Tabitha. I was curious and you answered my questions. So, there's nothing to apologize for."

"But you might have wanted to talk about the evening."

"You mean Horrible Helen?" he asked, his grin once again in place.

"Alex, she did do a superb job of interviewing you, which contributed to the excellent signing you had."

"I guess."

"You didn't like being the center of attention, did you?"

"Truthfully? No. I wanted to hide under the table."

Tabitha laughed. "Spoken like a true introvert!"

"Yeah, that's me."

"Well, it's late. I'll see you in the morning." She put her keycard in the lock, then turned back to him. "Do you want to work out in the morning or do you prefer to sleep in?"

"If you're going, wake me and I'll join you."

"All right. Good night."

When he made no move to open his own door,

Tabitha must have sensed his hesitation. "Is something wrong, Alex?"

"No. I—just wanted to thank you for staying with me today. I didn't handle everything very well, but you helped me." He reached out and caught her shoulders and kissed her on the cheek. "My way of saying thanks."

Then he disappeared into his room, closing the door behind him before she could tell what else he was thinking.

Chapter Four

After San Francisco, they traveled north to Seattle. Despite his first shaky day, Tabitha discovered Alex needed little guidance or support. He charmed the interviewers and had excellent sessions on both television and radio, but he continued to answer personal questions with generalities.

The second day in Seattle they finished early, and Tabitha suggested they take the ferry that ran among the San Juan Islands. Derek had visited there last year and raved about the islands. Leaving their car parked at the landing, they boarded the ferry and sat down in the passenger lounge, since the air was too crisp out on the water to remain outside.

When the ferry docked at its farthest point, Friday Harbor, they got off to walk around the town.

"Oh, I love it here!" Tabitha said, drawing in a deep breath.

"Would you want to live on an island?"

"Probably not. I wouldn't want to be so far from my family."

"I don't have that problem," Alex muttered. "And I certainly could be a hermit here. The view would be terrific."

"You don't have any family left?"

He shrugged. "My father and mother are still living, but we don't visit each other."

"Why?" she asked, horrified at the thought.

"Because neither of them learned to care about anyone but themselves. They are the antithesis of Jenny."

Tabitha stared at him blankly. His parents didn't care about him? She couldn't imagine her mother being like that. Even Joel, her new stepfather, would do anything for her and her sisters. All she could think to say was, "I'm sorry."

They awkwardly continued their walk, Tabitha trying unsuccessfully to think of something to say. Only when they entered a grocery store and she found his book, did she break through the wall of silence. "Alex, look, your book. That's exciting!"

"Yeah. Probably the first copy that's crossed the water. That's why I couldn't live here. In bad weather, there wouldn't be any mail delivery or maybe even telephone service. I wouldn't be able to leave if I wanted to. But you're right. It is charming."

In fact, they spent a delightful afternoon touring and talking, stopping for a drink at a tiny café on the shore.

On the ferry ride back, they even braved the wind for a short time on deck.

Once they got back to the hotel, they went to their rooms, not connecting this time, to freshen up for dinner. As soon as Tabitha opened her door, she noticed the red message light blinking on her phone. Checking the voice mail, she discovered she had a call from Tommie.

Hurriedly, she dialed Tommie's number. When her sister answered, she breathed a sigh of relief. She'd been afraid Tommie had gone into labor. "I assume you didn't call because you're having your baby?"

"No," Tommie replied, sounding disgusted. "The doctor said at least three more weeks."

"Hey, maybe I'll be there, after all. How are you feeling?"

"Fine. But I didn't call about me."

"Is it Teresa? Or the twins?"

"Everyone's fine. Look, Tabitha, I talked to Teresa and we both agreed you should know."

With a bad feeling, Tabitha asked, "Know what?"

"Derek called Mom. He was mad that you left when he'd made plans for the two of you. He called her to ask her to tell you he was moving on. He couldn't wait six weeks for you to come back."

Tabitha sat there, clutching the phone. She'd spoken to Derek after agreeing to take Mona's place, and though he wasn't overly thrilled by her opportunity, he seemed to understand. She remembered thinking how supportive he was. Apparently not. Apparently there was a lot about Derek she had misread.

Just as she'd misread many men before him. First Roger, then Tom.

Her sister picked up on the silence.

"He's no good, Tab. Anyone who would give up on you just because of six weeks wouldn't be there for the long haul. He's too self-centered. You don't want him!"

"No, I guess I don't. But I thought—"

"I know, honey. Teresa and I are going to look for someone for you while you're gone. I know it's hard to be alone."

"Don't bother. I'm—I'm fine, Tommie. Better to find out now than six months after I've married him." Her voice broke then, and she hurried off the phone, not wanting Tommie to pick up on it. "Thanks for calling me, Tommie, and take care. Bye."

She hung up before her sister could say any more. She needed to be alone, needed time to think. Sadness was her first distinguishable emotion. As she stood by the window looking out on Seattle, she finally let the tears fall. She finally let go of another dream.

Why did she always seem to attract men who only wanted to sleep with her? She was proud of her body, but that wasn't all she had to offer. She'd thought Derek had understood her and wanted to be with her. The real Tabitha Tyler. Obviously he'd changed his mind.

A creep. That was what Derek was—and what almost every man she'd ever dated was. Still, she knew good guys were out there. Tommie and Teresa had found them.

"Where's mine?" she asked the fates.

As if in reply, there was a knock on her door.

Alex. In her misery she'd forgotten about meeting him for dinner. Wiping away her tears, she went to open the door.

Much to her dismay, Alex took one look at her and knew something was wrong.

"Tabitha, what's wrong? Did you get bad news from home?"

"Not exactly. Well, sort of. Yeah," she finally admitted, bitterness now replacing the sadness in her voice.

"What happened? Do you need to leave?"

"No, don't be silly. It was just…something personal." Something she'd keep to herself. Grabbing her purse, she walked out the door. "Are you ready to go eat?"

"Yeah, but we can wait—"

"No, that's not necessary. Let's go."

They had decided to use the restaurant in the hotel, since they had an early-morning flight to Los Angeles. They wanted to get their packing done tonight, after dinner.

The elevator ride to the restaurant was a silent one. After they were seated, Alex took her hand and said, "Now, tell me why you were crying. You'll feel better if we talk about it."

"Is that your professional opinion, Doctor?" she asked, her voice a little stiff.

"That's what helped me. I hadn't talked to anyone about Jenny until you. You gave me some perspective and some healing."

Tabitha was happy she was able to help him. Perhaps he was right. Perhaps she should talk about it. "You remember me telling you about the man I was dating?"

"Was?"

"It seems six weeks without a woman to adore him is too much for Derek."

"So he's an idiot. You wouldn't want to be married to an idiot, would you?" With a grin, he added, "Think about your poor children."

A reluctant smile appeared on Tabitha's lips. "True. And if he got this upset over my taking on a job, it'd be impossible to keep him happy."

"He should be worrying about keeping you happy, not the other way around." He lifted Tabitha's hand to his lips. "I've only known you a few days, but I already know you're an extraordinary woman."

She felt a tingle from her hand right up her arm, and battled a blush that threatened to take over her cheek. Last night when he'd kissed her by the hotel-room door, she'd had the same reaction, but her better judgment had warned her that Alex's kiss had meant nothing more than a thank-you. One human reaching out to another.

Was this the same? That familiar inner voice told her so, yet she couldn't help reacting to it. Probably, she told herself, because her ego had just taken a beating at the hands of Derek.

Instinctively she knew Alex would never treat a woman like that. Never treat her like that. And it wasn't just the Alex who wrote such a touching, tender book, but the flesh-and-blood man who sat next to her. She looked at him, as if he were suddenly revealed to her.

"Thank you, Alex." She squeezed his hand. "I'll admit, I had some doubts about Derek..." Doubts she'd never voiced to anyone, not even her sisters. Tommie and Teresa had been there to nurse her through her previous bad relationships, but this time it was different. They were happily married, building their families. Which was what she wanted so badly she'd overlooked Derek's flaws.

She shared that insight with Alex. "I suppose my vision was cloudy."

"A lot of times we make decisions based on what we want it to be, rather than the reality of the situation. Especially in marriage. Women think they can change their husbands once they marry them, and men don't see the work that goes into always looking beautiful. They assume that once she takes on all the chores his mother has been doing for him, everything will continue as when they were dating."

"My sisters' husbands are very supportive. Jim takes care of the babies as much as Teresa does. And Pete is doing all the cooking now that Tommie is so close to time."

"And that's the way it should be." After a moment of silence, Alex said, "I wanted to have children, though I had uncertainties about my role as a father. But I put it off too long. I wish—" He stopped, but Tabitha knew that he was about to say.

"I know," she said, squeezing his hand.

That move seemed to remind him they were holding hands. He pulled his away and awkwardly cleared his throat. "Anyway, I'm sorry things turned out this way for you."

"You've certainly had more than your share of heartache, losing a perfect marriage after three years of bliss."

Alex frowned, but the waiter brought their food and the conversation ended. A few minutes passed till he spoke again. "I may have exaggerated Jenny's perfection a little. She was human, not perfect. She made mistakes, but she always cared, always tried. And I loved her."

"I know. I had a friend in high school who died of cancer. We were best friends, shared a lot of likes and dislikes. I was almost as close to her as I was to my sisters. After she died, everyone talked about what a perfect person she was. I hated that! It was like I'd lost who she really was."

"Yeah. I think I may have done that myself in writing the book. I couldn't bring myself to indicate any fault in Jenny. The harder I tried to deify her, the more I lost her. Only this week, as I've begun to recognize her as a person, to remember her little faults, has she come back to me."

"I'm glad." She gave him a genuine smile. Then, in an attempt to get away from their problems, she said, "Now, I'm going to have baked Alaska for dessert, in honor of being so close to Alaska and despite the workout I'm going to have to do later."

"Good idea. I'll join you."

"In the dessert or the workout?" she asked.

"Both!" And he waved for their waiter.

Hollywood was quite different from Seattle.

"How long are we scheduled to be here?" Alex asked after their first day of interviews.

"Three days. Mona says L.A. is a hotbed of readers."

"Okay," Alex said, sounding weary.

"Running out of steam?"

"Not that, exactly. But it's hot and crowded anywhere we go, and most of the people seem plastic. I haven't seen so many perky breasts since I was in high school!"

"Dr. Myerson!" Tabitha proclaimed, pretending shock.

"Miss Tyler!" he returned. "Haven't you seen enough muscle yet? Do we need to take you to the beach this afternoon?"

"We don't have time to waste on the beach," she said primly.

"That's a relief. I don't understand how anyone can remain normal in a world where everyone strives for perfection."

"That's why I'm along. You can look at me and know everyone's not perfect," she teased.

He smiled at her. "I don't think so."

"Thank you kindly. You fell right into my trap to get a compliment out of you."

They were in a cab on the way back to the hotel after their third interview of the day. He reached over and clasped her hand in his. "I'll have to hold on tight, though. I thought we were going to have another Helen on our hands with that last lady. She kept patting my leg every time we took a commercial break."

"Well, she *was* beautiful."

"Yeah, but you'd make a better mother. Tell you what. I'll give you my phone number. When you get ready to have a baby, if you can't find anyone you want, call me. I'll volunteer!"

Tabitha smiled and because they had fallen into a teasing relationship said, "So you're saying I can't find someone on my own?"

"Not a chance, lady. I'm saying you might not find what you want. So maybe you'd take me," he finished with a grin.

"So now I'm supposed to pay you a compliment? Payback time? Oh, thank you, Dr. Myerson! I'd love to have your baby!" she exclaimed in overly dramatic tones.

When they both caught the taxi driver's startled look, they burst into laughter.

Fortunately, they reached the hotel in a minute and hurriedly left the cab, but Tabitha gave the driver an extra-large tip. "I'm going to ruin Mona's budget if we don't stop carrying on in front of the cab drivers."

"Don't worry about it. You're doing a great job. You should think about doing this for a living."

That was exactly what Mona had said when she'd talked to her the other day. She told Alex of their conversation. "Mona wants to expand and she thinks if this trip is successful, she'll have the business." But Tabitha wasn't sure publicity tours were for her, despite how much she was enjoying this one.

Alex gave her a vote of confidence. "You'd be great at it."

"Thanks. I'm still committed to teaching, but it's nice to have options. So, do you want to eat dinner now and then work out in the morning?"

"That sounds good. I want to talk to you about something one of the callers said today."

"What was that?"

"She suggested I write a romance novel. Said my book was better than any of the romance novels she'd read lately."

"I can see that possibility in your book. Now you'll have to come up with a plot and characters."

"You're a writing expert too?"

"No, but Teresa is. She's going to have her book published. It's for children." Teresa had been offered a contract shortly after the twins were born.

"Do you read romance novels?"

"Yes, I do."

"Why do you sound so defensive?" he asked.

"Because sometimes men think if you read romance, you must be dumb."

"So why do you read it?"

"It's very entertaining and emotional. And it has the happy ending women want. It empowers women too."

"Good answers. Come on. We'll discuss my future over dinner."

Tabitha's hotel-room phone rang about ten-thirty several nights and a couple of cities later. Now they were in Denver. Figuring no one would call that late unless it was an emergency, she grabbed it at once. "Hello?"

"Tabitha, I need you to come here."

"Alex? Is that you? What do you need?"

"Your advice. Have you gone to bed?"

"Not yet, but I was thinking about it. I thought maybe it was my family calling." Her heart was still beating fast.

"I'm sorry, I didn't realize it was this late." He paused, then said, "I guess this can wait until tomorrow."

"I'm still dressed, Alex. I can come."

"Great! I'll see you in five minutes."

He didn't sound as sorry as he had a minute earlier. Tabitha was pretty sure she'd been had. But keeping him happy was her job. And after that first day, the job had gotten a lot easier. So she went to bed half an hour later. That would be all right.

She went up two floors and knocked on his door.

As if he'd been waiting for her, he swung the door wide at once. "Come in."

"What's up?"

"I've written a synopsis, my first one. Remember that book I bought about writing? That's the first thing it said I should do."

She remembered the book because he'd had his nose buried in it between his interviews.

"Okay, good. What do you need me for?"

"I thought maybe you'd read it for me."

Tabitha took a step back, protesting, "Alex, I don't know anything about a synopsis. I've only read the finished product."

"I know, but I don't have anyone else to ask. Not until I get home and I can show my agent. Provided he knows anything about romances," he qualified.

"I guess I can take a look at it, but I don't know how helpful my opinion will be."

That didn't deter Alex's enthusiasm. He pulled out a chair and ushered her to it. "Great. Here, sit down.

Want me to go get you a soda? Or order a pot of coffee?"

Since he was in such an accommodating mood, she asked for a piece of chocolate cake. They hadn't had dessert at dinner. "The cake would be good with the decaf coffee," she said sweetly. She didn't worry about him paying for it. It would go on Mona's tab.

He immediately did as she asked, but he kept his eyes on her as she took the pages he offered and settled in a chair near one of the lamps. After he'd placed the order, he sat on the bed and pretended indifference. But Tabitha noticed he watched her out of the corner of his eyes.

After about three pages, she went back to the second page to check on a fact.

"Is something wrong with it?" he asked, leaning forward with a frown.

"No, Alex. I just wanted to be sure I was remembering correctly."

Five minutes later the coffee and cake were delivered. Since she only had a couple more pages to read, she told Alex she'd eat when she finished. After reading the last page, she put the papers down and walked over to the room-service tray.

She poured herself a cup of coffee and sipped it, feeling its warmth down her throat. Then she took a forkful of the cake and closed her eyes to savor the rich chocolate.

The sensory experience came to an abrupt end when a loud voice bellowed from across the room. "Tabitha, if you make me wait any longer, I'm going to wring your neck!"

Chapter Five

Alex reached over and snatched the plate from her lap. "No more cake until you talk."

"Spoilsport!" she cried. Then she smiled. "I think you've got a great story."

He heaved a big sigh. "You're not just saying that?"

"No, but I do have a couple of suggestions for you to consider." She went through the outline, offering her ideas, then when she neared the end, said, "I think your black moment needs to be stronger."

"Black moment?"

"Every romance novel has a black moment, the moment where the heroine or hero must make a decision that could possibly end their relationship. Of course one or the other comes up with a solution that allows their happiness."

"Hmmm. I hadn't thought of that. It would make it a

stronger book, wouldn't it?" He reached for his pages but she refused to release them. "Is there something else?"

"Yes, my cake. I'll trade you."

"Deal," he agreed with a grin, handing her the plate.

She ate her cake and finished her coffee, thinking about how relaxed they were now. It was such a difference from their difficult beginning.

She could easily understand why all the interviewers had enjoyed talking to him. Even Mona, to whom she'd sent tapes, had remarked on the easy rapport Alex had established with the reporters.

As for their personal connection, Alex had offered to skip tomorrow's interview and take a drive up into the Rockies, a part of the country neither of them had been to previously. As much as Tabitha was tempted to spend a relaxing day with Alex, she refused. She didn't want to mess up on the tour, not when Mona was counting on her.

It was late, and they did have another long day ahead, so she stood up to take her leave. "If you don't need me anymore, I'm going to bed."

Alex stood and without warning reached out to envelop her in a hug. "Thank you, Tabitha. I don't think I could've written this without you."

Surprised by her reaction, she stiffened and backed out of the embrace. "Of course you could. You're a wonderful writer." Then hurrying out the door, she threw over her shoulder, "Good night."

"I'll see you in the gym in the morning?" Alex called out.

"Yeah," she said without turning around. "I'll call you."

When she finally closed the door behind her, she let out the breath she didn't know she'd been holding. Where had that reaction come from? Sure, Alex had surprised her by hugging her, but she was even more astounded by how much she'd enjoyed the feel of his rock-hard chest and strong arms. By how much she wanted to hug him back, to melt into his arms. To stay in his arms.

It was just a friendly gesture, she told herself. Alex meant nothing else by it. And she'd do well to remember that.

Besides, it would be suicidal to fall for Alex Myerson. His heart belonged to Jenny, and it always would.

Alex got ready for bed, his mind focused on the story he'd devised. He couldn't wait to start writing it. It was a good thing he had Tabitha with him. He wasn't sure Mona had ever read a romance.

Now if he could only bring the characters to life. Writing another book would give him something to focus on. He'd finished the book about Jenny almost a year ago. Since then, with the exception of his limited practice, he'd rattled around the house he'd bought for her, going crazy.

Now he had something to concentrate on. And Tabitha to help him. For four more weeks.

But, he realized, their friendship didn't have to end when they went home. They both lived in Fort Worth. He could call her, or take her out to dinner.

Not as a date, of course. Dating would be a betrayal of Jenny. But Tabitha was a wonderful person. He'd loved spending time with her, talking to her. And hugging her…as a friend, of course. And she was a good traveling companion. In fact, after he finished this project, he thought about going to Europe. He hadn't been since college. Maybe he'd ask Tabitha to go with him. She'd have his protection and they knew already they traveled well together. As he'd learned with Jenny, a moment shared was more enjoyable than being alone.

He should know.

Next stop, Chicago.

Tabitha waited until she reached her room to look more than one day ahead. She was growing a little weary of the constant travel. She'd always thought it would be so exciting.

Her tour had been exciting to her. Now that she saw it from Mona's perspective, she realized it was hard work. And hard on the body. Since they had no activities tonight, she decided to work out before dinner. If they had an early day tomorrow, she thought as she pulled out the file on Chicago, she wouldn't have to get up so early.

She blinked twice and looked at the schedule again. Tomorrow was an open day. Odd, since they'd had something scheduled every day since they left Fort Worth. Maybe Mona knew they would need a break. She went to call her and thank her, but the phone rang.

"How about dinner?" It was Alex. "I'm starved."

She automatically checked her watch. It was almost

six. "Okay, give me ten minutes and let's go to something simple. I don't want to dress up."

"Sure. The bellhop says there's a real Chicago pizza place around the corner."

"All right. I'll come to your room in ten minutes."

"Hurry!" he ordered, but she could hear the teasing in his voice.

She hurriedly changed, promising herself she'd call Mona when she got back.

Nine minutes later she reached Alex's room, wearing slacks and a short-sleeve sweater, her hair pulled back into a ponytail.

"I'm glad you were fast," Alex said when he opened the door. "I was about to start chewing on the bedspread!"

"You're exaggerating, Alex. It hasn't been that long since our lunch in Denver." She smiled and started back to the elevator.

"Hey, you look like a teenager in that get-up."

She looked at him over her shoulder. "Thanks, I guess." But his words brought a smile to her lips. Leading a publicity tour was hard work, but Alex had made it easier.

The sidewalks were crowded and Alex took hold of her arm to guide her. It was a gentlemanly thing to do, a protective act. Tabitha smiled, pleased with his gentle care of her. But she still couldn't calm the nervous flutter in her stomach whenever he touched her.

When they reached the restaurant, a noisy, cheerful place, Tabitha finally relaxed. This place was perfect for a friendly dinner. They split a pizza, both choosing the toppings they wanted.

If she was weary of the tour, Alex must be exhausted. He was the one who had to face the interviewers. Maybe that was Mona's brilliance, providing a break in the middle of the tour.

"I have a surprise for you," she said, sipping her diet soda while they waited for their pizza.

"Good, I like surprises," Alex said, smiling at her.

"We have tomorrow completely free."

He froze, his smile disappearing. "What's the date?"

"June eighteenth. Why? What's wrong? You don't want a day off?" She stared at him, surprised by his reaction.

"I don't want to talk about it." Abruptly, he stood and walked out of the restaurant without a word, startling the waiter who had just arrived with their pizza.

"If it's not too much trouble," Tabitha told him apologetically. "I need the pizza boxed up to go."

While she waited, she sat alone at the table, feeling conspicuous. Her mind frantically tried to figure out his reaction. Then she reached in her purse and pulled out her cell phone. Before she could dial Mona's number, the waiter returned with the pizza.

"Thank you so much," she said, paying the bill and adding an extra tip. Then she walked back to the hotel.

When she knocked on Alex's door, a voice, rough with emotion, called out, "Go away."

"I'm leaving your pizza here if you want it. Good night."

As she walked down the hallway to the elevator, she kept turning to see if he opened his door. When he finally did, she managed to step onto the elevator without him seeing her.

At least she wouldn't worry about him not eating.

Back in her room, she picked up the phone and called Mona. After their initial greeting, Mona asked, "How's it going?"

"I'm not sure exactly. Why did you schedule a complete off-day tomorrow?"

"What's the date?" Mona asked.

"June eighteenth," Tabitha said, her apprehension rising at the tension in Mona's voice.

"Oh, damn," Mona muttered, sounding discouraged. "I'm sorry, Tabitha. I should've told you. I've screwed everything up."

Tabitha knew that wasn't true. Mona had planned a great tour. It had been rough the first couple of days, but things had gone well since. "Just tell me, Mona. We'll take care of whatever is wrong."

"It's his wedding anniversary," Mona whispered. "He told me he couldn't work on that day. I figured I'd deal with it when we got there. Besides, a day's rest never hurt anyone."

"You're right. I'll enjoy a day off, too."

"I know he hasn't been easy. You haven't said anything, but I know he—he's fixated on his dead wife."

"True, but he's performed well, so that's all we have to worry about."

"All right. Let me know what happens."

"I will, Mona. Don't worry. Everything will be all right."

Wouldn't it?

* * *

How could he?

He'd told Mona he'd have to have his anniversary off. It was a special day. They'd had to travel on the one-year anniversary of Jenny's death. That was when he'd been so difficult with Tabitha.

When he'd heard her announcing she was leaving his pizza outside the door, he couldn't believe she'd be so thoughtful, since he'd left her alone in the restaurant.

He shouldn't eat any of it. He deserved to go without food. Except that thought was so masochistic. He knew because he'd had patients like that, denying themselves any pleasure or even any necessity.

Slowly, he opened the pizza box and took a deep breath of the aroma. Hungry, he took a bite of the pizza and chewed it slowly. Heaven! No, not heaven. It was good food, that was all.

What really bothered him more than anything was that he'd completely forgotten his and Jenny's anniversary. He'd begun to enjoy his tour, enjoy his time with Tabitha.

He supposed he was vulnerable because he hadn't been around the opposite sex for a year. Hell, he'd hardly been around anyone, male or female. He felt like a long-starved plant suddenly watered at regular intervals and given plant food, too. He'd bloomed.

But he didn't believe he should.

Normally, when he spoke to his patients, he asked them to tell him what their dead partner would want for them. Now that he had a greater understanding of the people he'd treated, he didn't want to answer that question.

When he finished his pizza, he thought he should call Tabitha and apologize. But the fact that he wanted to, so badly, told him it was a bad idea. He'd thank her when he saw her. Which would probably be the day after tomorrow.

Tabitha didn't see or hear from her client the next day. Rather than worry herself sick about him, she exercised in the morning and then had a massage, which eased her stiff muscles from all the airplane rides.

After lunch, she got a manicure and pedicure. By the end of the day, she felt thoroughly pampered. Then she stopped in a bookstore and found a romance by her favorite author. She couldn't think of a better way to spend the evening.

She'd gone over their schedule for the next day. Work out at seven-thirty, have breakfast at eight-thirty, leave by nine. Since their first interview wasn't until ten o'clock, they'd get there a half hour before the interview, which most of the producers preferred.

It was tempting to call Alex this evening to be sure he would show up in the morning. But she wouldn't do that. He'd asked for the day off…and he was going to get it.

By nightfall on his free day, Alex was restless. He'd stayed in his room all day, ordering room service for every meal. Focusing his thoughts on Jenny, as he'd done when she was alive. He felt he'd brought himself back into focus. There'd be no more being distracted by the pretty blonde a couple of floors up.

But he felt he should check on her. After all, a pretty young woman on her own should be careful. He felt responsible for her. He picked up the phone and dialed her room number.

No answer.

Fine, so she had found something to do without him. That was just as well. He wouldn't worry about her until the morning. With a copy of the schedule, he planned his time in the morning to include a workout—whether *she* showed up or not. After all, he didn't need a baby-sitter!

Tabitha listened to the phone ringing on the other end in Alex's room, wondering what she'd do if he'd checked out of the hotel. Or was drunk in some bar.

"Hello?" Alex answered, out of breath.

"Dr. Myerson, are you all right?"

"I'm fine. I was just leaving."

"Where are you going?"

"To work out."

"Good. I'll be up there in a few minutes."

"Fine." And he hung up the phone.

"The same to you!" she exclaimed into the dead phone. It was as if they'd returned to those early days of the tour. No problem. She could handle it.

Slipping into her exercise clothes, she hurried up to the gym. Even after her workout, she still couldn't find Alex. She used the phone in the gym to call down to his room.

"Dr. Myerson, do you want me to order breakfast for both of us?" she asked when he finally answered.

"No, thank you. I've already ordered."

"All right. We'll need to leave at nine."

"I'll meet you in the lobby."

Again he hung up on her.

She hurried to her room, showered and dressed, then went down to the coffee shop on the ground floor and ordered her breakfast, facing the lobby of the hotel.

Just finishing her second cup of coffee as Alex got off the elevator, Tabitha paid her bill and met him in the lobby.

"Ready?" she asked, keeping her voice calm.

"Yes. I can go on my own, if you're too busy."

Glaring at him, she said, "No, I think I can work it into my schedule." Then she strolled out the hotel door as if she had all the time in the world. She waved for a taxi and got in before she looked to see if Alex had followed her.

He got in after her but remained silent.

"Did you have a good breakfast?" she asked casually to break the ice.

"Fine."

She opened her briefcase and pulled out a file. "The interviewer this morning is Jack Gray. His show is a mixture of interviews and entertainment. I believe you're scheduled after a singer, but I'll recheck that as soon as we get there."

"Fine."

"Your segment will run about ten minutes. Did you review the questions he submitted? I don't think they'll be a problem."

"Fine."

As the cab pulled to the curb, she said, "I hope you're

saving all your conversation for the interview. If you answer all the questions with 'fine,' then we might as well go home."

"Fi—" He stopped before he could say it, and just glared at her.

Drawing a deep breath, she suddenly mourned the past days of camaraderie they'd shared. They were at the halfway mark, but it appeared the rest of the trip would be a cold war.

Two days later they arrived in Detroit. Tabitha sent their luggage in a taxi to the hotel, to be placed in their rooms. She and Alex would register after the interview. Then they got in a cab to get to the TV studio.

Tabitha didn't brief Alex on the interview. She'd given him the information she had before he returned to his room in Chicago last night to order his dinner to his room. They hadn't shared a meal since the pizza, which they hadn't even eaten together.

Once they reached the studio, she talked to the director and introduced Alex to him. When she asked where Daniel Garcia, the interviewer, was, the director smiled. "He doesn't usually come in until about five minutes before the show begins."

When Tabitha frowned, he hurriedly added, "But he is completely prepared."

"Good," Tabitha said calmly.

Alex stood there, saying nothing.

"Alex, would you like something to drink while you're waiting?" Tabitha asked.

"Oh!" the director exclaimed. "Oh, I'm sorry. Yes,

Dr. Myerson, we have coffee and donuts and sodas. Whatever you want."

"Thanks, Bill," Alex said, as if Bill were his best friend. "It's been a long day. I'd like a donut and coffee, please."

"Right away, Doc."

As soon as the director moved away, Tabitha whispered, "Must you make it sound like I have you beaten at regular intervals?"

He gave her a cool smile and looked away.

She could've warned him that at two in the afternoon, the donuts were not going to be too fresh. But why should she worry about his comfort? Let him suffer.

Tabitha stepped behind the set, looking for Mr. Garcia's dressing room. She found a room with his name on it and knocked softly.

"What is it?" a man growled.

Great! Two grumps. She cautiously opened the door slightly, only to discover the man seated in front of a mirror, with another man combing his hair.

"Mr. Garcia?" she said softly. "I'm Tabitha Tyler, the publicist accompanying Dr. Myerson. I thought I should check with you before the show. He's looked at your questions and doesn't have a problem with them."

"Thanks for nothing!" he growled again.

The hairstylist rushed to the door. "Thank you, Miss Tyler. We got the advanced material. I'm going over it with him now. He'll be up to par by show time."

"Thank you," she said softly, pleased with the man's graciousness.

"And I apologize for his bad attitude. He got to bed late, er, early this morning."

"I understand."

How could she complain about no one controlling Garcia? She certainly couldn't control Alex.

When she returned to the sound stage, Alex was sitting in one of the canvas chairs behind the camera, holding a cup of coffee and a donut, one in each hand.

She strolled over and looked at the donut, with one bite out of it. "You'd better eat it in a hurry so you'll be able to clear your throat before the interview," she said pleasantly.

"Here," he said and shoved the donut toward her.

"Five minutes," the director called. "Someone drag Garcia out of his dressing room!"

"Oh, great," Alex muttered.

Tabitha continued to smile, enjoying his discomfort.

The director yelled several more times. Finally, at one minute to air time, Garcia came out of his room, clutching a large coffee cup.

"Is the singer here?" the director yelled.

"She hasn't shown up," one of his underlings reported.

"Okay, list the doctor first." The director turned to Alex. "Ready, Doc? We need you to go first. Go sit on the sofa across from Garcia."

With a frown, Alex did as he was told, but he wasn't happy about it.

The introductory music, on tape, signaled the beginning of the show. Garcia transformed himself into a smiling, happy man.

As soon as the music died down, he introduced Alex and got his pedigree correct, much to Tabitha's surprise. Then he immediately launched into a question about Alex's book.

After Alex gave a brief summation, Daniel Garcia leaned closer and began another question.

Just about that time a man dashed across the stage, stopping in front of the two men. "Shut up! Shut up!" he yelled.

"Get that man out of there," the director whispered. But the intruder must've heard him.

"Don't touch me. I've got a right to talk," the man said in a high, shrill voice as he spun around, ready to pounce.

Chapter Six

A harsh silence filled the normally busy area.

Tabitha could scarcely breathe, praying this scene wouldn't ruin Alex's interview. It had been going so well.

Quietly, calmly, Alex addressed the man, "Hello, I'm Alex Myerson. I don't believe I've met you."

"I'm—I'm Curtis Chambers." The man drew a deep breath and then shouted, "Don't move!" as Garcia attempted to slide away.

"It's all right, Curtis," Alex said. "Mr. Garcia isn't going to leave." His voice held a warning, but he didn't move his gaze from Chambers to Garcia. "Sit down on the end of the couch, so you can get comfortable."

Tabitha heard the director talking to the men in the control room.

"Call nine-one-one and tell them what's going on."

Tabitha leaned over and whispered, "No sirens."

The director jerked his head up and stared at her. Then he added, "No sirens."

Tabitha tried to step closer to the stage, but the director grabbed her arm. "Stay back."

She obeyed him, hoping to do what was right. But she strained to hear the ongoing conversation.

Alex smiled gently at the man, who looked crazed and irrational. "Curtis, why are you here?"

"I'm here to tell everyone that he's a bastard!" the man exclaimed, standing up and pointing at Garcia, who pressed back against his chair.

"Sit down, Curtis, and explain why," Alex invited. Once again the man sat on the edge of the sofa.

"Because he disrespected my wife and made her cry. She…died a couple of days later." Now his hysteria mixed with sadness, and tears ran down his face.

"How did he disrespect your wife, Curtis?"

"She wanted—wanted to enter a contest for best housewife. She—she was a wonderful housewife. But she was…big. And he made fun of her!"

"On the air?" Alex asked.

"No! No, I didn't!" Garcia protested.

"No, not on air. But she heard him making jokes about her size afterward." The man glared at Garcia.

"So you think you have to defend your wife's honor?" Alex asked quietly. "How do you want to defend her honor?"

The man looked unsure of himself. Then he said, "I have to. I failed her. I didn't protect her from his mean remarks!" He nodded toward Garcia. "He needs to pay!"

"I agree," Alex said. "But you have to figure out what you want in order to settle things. I don't think your wife would want you to be arrested on her behalf."

"I didn't deserve her!"

"We seldom do. My wife died, too, Curtis, and she was wonderful, too. But we don't get to make too many choices about life. All we can do is the best we can. Did your wife know you loved her?"

"Of course! I told her over and over how wonderful she was!"

"Then you did the best thing you could do for your wife. There are always bad people in the world. But the love we share insulates us from their hatred."

The man said nothing and Tabitha looked around her. The entire crew was staring at the sound stage with its spotlights. It was a surreal experience, as if they were watching a drama in a theater.

Curtis said, "Yes, but I still think he shouldn't have been so mean. He puts on a front, smiling on camera, and people think he's wonderful, but he's not. He's got everything in the world. Why did he have to be mean to my Ruth?"

As Alex drew a deep breath, preparing to answer him, Garcia spoke. "No, I don't! I don't have everything. I don't have anyone. My wife left me. I've been in a lot of pain, but I've had to hide it, be cheerful all the time and—and I can't!" he exclaimed, tears staining his cheeks, too.

"Did you know that?" one of the crew whispered to the director.

He shook his head no.

"You're just saying that to make me feel bad!" Curtis shouted.

"No, I'm not! We'd been married five years. I—I thought everything was fine. But she—she was having an affair and she left me for him." Garcia covered his eyes as tears streamed down his face.

"When did she leave you, Daniel?" asked Alex, the only one not crying.

"Three weeks ago. Curtis's wife came for the competition the next week. I was angry but I couldn't show it. But once the lights went off, I used my anger on some of the women, not to hurt them, just to—to get rid of the anger."

Alex and Curtis continued to stare at him, saying nothing.

"But I shouldn't have taken my anger out on those women. I'm sorry."

Just when Tabitha thought they were going to have a happy ending, there was a rush of footsteps and men shouting behind them.

Immediately, Curtis turned toward the noise. "Stay away! I want him to finish apologizing for my Ruth!" He leaped to his feet again.

"Sssh!" Tabitha hoped they would pay attention to her warning.

Alex tried to calm Curtis again. "Sit down, Curtis. I think we can solve this without the police," he said in a soothing voice, but his gaze was fixed beyond Curtis's shoulder.

Tabitha felt sure he was staring at her, sending a message. But she'd already gotten the message. She turned to the two policemen who had arrived. "Please," she whispered, "Dr. Myerson has the situation under control. Can you please wait?"

"Ma'am, I'm not sure—" the first officer began. The other policeman touched his arm and stopped him.

"We can check with our captain. What kind of doctor is Dr. Myerson?"

"He's a psychologist."

"Go in the control booth and call your captain," the director whispered.

"What's going on?" Curtis demanded, staring wildly around him.

"Curtis, you're all right. If you'll listen to me, I think we can resolve this without hurting you or Daniel." Alex drew a deep breath. "I don't believe you really want to cause problems. Daniel has already apologized to you. I'm sure he would apologize to Ruth now if he could. What more do you want?"

"I—I don't know. I wanted Ruth to know—"

"She knows, Curtis. But I can't believe she wants you in jail, or Daniel to be destroyed because of his remarks."

Suddenly Tabitha had an idea. She whispered to the director, who, after a moment, nodded vehemently. She stepped forward toward the stage. "Curtis?"

"Who is that?"

"Tabitha," Alex urged, "stay back."

Instead she stepped into the lighted area. "Curtis, I'm Dr. Myerson's publicist. I realize you don't want to make money because of Ruth's pain. But I think it would be good for you if you committed to several hours with a psychologist in the area."

"Can't afford it!" Curtis yelled.

"Perhaps not. But the station could. And Daniel could come with you. The two of you could talk out your problems and feel better about what has happened today."

Curtis stared at her without speaking. Finally he said, "That makes sense."

"And I think you could make a difference for other men out there if you and Daniel discussed your feelings on several shows to show your ongoing growth. They do makeovers all the time on television. You could be the ultimate makeover, from the inside out. You could show people how to deal with their pain and suffering, as you'll learn to do." Tabitha drew a deep breath. "Then Ruth's suffering won't have been in vain."

Complete silence surrounded Tabitha and she had no idea if Curtis would accept her proposal. She waited patiently, her gaze only shifting occasionally to Alex.

"I—I might agree to that," Curtis said, his voice low. He turned to Alex. "What do you think, Doc?"

"I think it's a wonderful idea. Both you and Daniel are suffering. What better way to end your pain than to help others. Right, Daniel?"

"Right...if the director thinks—"

"I think it's a great idea. The station is behind it," the director announced out loud.

"Then okay, I'll agree to that."

"I think the two of you will come out of this well." Alex held out his hand, waiting for Curtis's decision.

"But, Doc, what if—what if I don't deserve—"

"Everyone deserves to learn how to handle pain,

Curtis. Remember, Ruth loved you. That's how you know you deserve to be treated."

"Yeah, okay." Curtis extended his hand.

As Alex shook it, he said, "Thank you, Curtis."

The policemen stepped on the stage and Curtis panicked. "You tricked me! You tricked me!" he shrieked and struggled with the two officers.

"Stop!" Alex said, rising. "I promised this man he'd receive treatment."

The director took off his headset and joined them on the stage. "We don't want an arrest. We've made promises and we intend to keep them. Please release him."

"You don't want to press charges?" one of the policemen asked.

"No. We're going to help both these men learn to deal with their pain and anger and we're going to broadcast their progress to help others." The director grinned, enjoying his generosity since it might mean big ratings.

Tabitha edged her way around the sound stage until she was standing near Alex. He reached out a hand and Tabitha took it, relieved that the situation seemed to have a happy ending.

"We have to at least warn him about trespassing."

Curtis nodded. "I know I shouldn't have trespassed, but I had to avenge my wife."

"Since these people agree, I doubt you'll have to go to jail. You got lucky," the second policeman said.

Curtis, after being released, turned to Alex. "Thank you, Doc. I would've messed up big-time if you hadn't been kind to me."

"I'm glad I could help," Alex said.

"But how did your wife die?" Daniel Garcia demanded. "I didn't really kill her, did I?"

"No. But she was so unhappy...she died in a car accident two days later. It just all ran together in my head. I guess I wasn't thinking too clearly."

"Man, I'm sorry, Curtis. Really, I am," Daniel said, tears again rolling down his cheeks.

The director asked Curtis to meet with Tabitha and their own publicity people, while Alex and Daniel did the show again. "We'll tape it for tomorrow."

Curtis looked at Alex. "You think I can believe them?"

"You can believe Tabitha. She won't lie to you."

Tabitha heard his quiet words and her heart swelled with pride. Alex trusted her. That meant a lot. She released Alex's hand and came to the end of the couch. "Shall we go, Curtis? It will work out okay."

Curtis stared at her hand in surprise. Then he wiped his hand on his jeans and took hers. "Okay."

She led him away to the room where the publicity people were waiting.

Alex watched Tabitha walk away with Curtis. He believed what he'd said. He could trust Tabitha.

"Need a break before we tape, Dr. Myerson?" Bill, the director, asked.

"Yes, please. A glass of water would be nice, and I think I'd better have a few minutes with Daniel."

But Daniel seemed eager to leave the set. "I—I was going to go to my dressing room."

"That's fine, Daniel. I wanted to make sure you were all right. That was an emotional scene."

"Yeah. You know, I've always popped off, used my mouth to get me out of trouble, but—well, I appreciate what you did, Dr. Myerson."

"Thanks. I'll see you in a few minutes."

Daniel Garcia hurried away from the sound stage.

Alex rose from the sofa. "Is there somewhere I can sit without being under the spotlights?" he asked Bill.

"Sure. In the greenroom. I think you'll find some cookies in there too."

"Thank you."

Alex didn't find anything to eat in the greenroom, but he didn't care. He could use some peace and quiet. That had been a dangerous situation, in spite of how quickly he'd talked Curtis down. At any moment Curtis might have lost control and attacked Daniel.

Alex had lost a patient to suicide before, and he never wanted to do so again. He feared that would have been Curtis's choice if they hadn't intervened. He'd certainly demonstrated the signs. Alex's mind dwelled on the situation, and a new determination rose in him. He might continue writing the romance novel; he'd been enjoying it. But first he had to write another book to help others. *Rejoining the Human Race*. The re-entry was scary but worth the trip.

His re-entry had gone smoothly because of Tabitha.

A young man entered with bottled water and a plate of cookies. "Here you are, sir," he said deferentially.

"Thanks." He took a cookie from the plate. "Hey, they're warm. Did you have one?"

The young man's eyes widened and he shook his head.

"Sit down and have a cookie with me," Alex offered. Suddenly he didn't want to be alone anymore.

When Tabitha got out of the meeting, Alex had already left for his signing. He'd sent her word that he'd be okay, for her to continue the meeting.

The director came over to shake her hand. "I want to thank you personally for helping out today. Your ideas were great. If you ever need a job, you've got one here, or I'll provide a reference for you, too."

"Thank you, Bill, that's very kind. But I already have several jobs," she said with a laugh. "So did the taping go okay?"

"Yeah, it did. Daniel was really into the subject after his breakdown. I think we did a great show."

"Good. I've got to get to Alex's signing before it ends. Thanks again," she said as she hurried out of the studio. Grabbing a taxi, she was quickly carried to the bookstore where Alex was signing. To her surprise, the line went halfway around the block.

She got to the door, but a woman there thought she was trying to cut in. "No, you don't. I've waited in line for an hour. You're not getting ahead of me."

"I wasn't trying to. I'm Dr. Myerson's publicist. I need to talk to him."

"You promise?" the woman demanded.

"Yes. My name is Tabitha Tyler. Here, you come with me. Your wait is over," she assured the woman, taking her by the hand. They approached the table where Alex was signing and conversing with his fans.

"Alex? This lady thought I was trying to cut in line, so I brought her with me to get her book signed. Could you do that for me?"

"I'm glad you're here," he said even as he reached for the lady's book. "Good evening, Miss…"

"Joy Stevens is my name, Dr. Myerson. I certainly do appreciate this. We're all so glad that man didn't hurt you."

"Me, too," Alex said, flashing his beautiful smile.

Tabitha figured the woman wouldn't forget that smile for a while. After Joy had left Alex, Tabitha leaned down. "Is everything all right? Can I get you anything?"

"No, I'm fine. Did the meeting go well?"

"Yes. I'll tell you about it over dinner," she said with a smile. Then she remembered they weren't sharing meals anymore. "I mean, whenever—"

"Over dinner," he said firmly, as if there were no doubt.

Dinner was a return to normal in Tabitha's mind. They enjoyed their meal, discussing the day's events. They had a lot to talk about, but she noticed that Alex carefully skirted any of his own emotions when Curtis had stood before him.

"Weren't you upset?" she finally asked.

"Weren't you, when you chose to intervene when you thought you could help?"

"Yes, somewhat, but I didn't really think he'd agree."

"I wasn't convinced!" Alex muttered, glaring at her.

"You're mad at me?"

"I didn't want you to put yourself at risk."

"But it was okay for you to sit there and calmly discuss Curtis's emotions?"

"No one would've mourned me if I'd been hurt today. You, on the other hand…"

"You're wrong!" Tabitha actually covered her mouth with her hand, not having intended to protest. But she couldn't help herself. She'd learned today how excruciatingly painful it would be to her to live in a world without Alex in it. She was still reeling from the revelation that she had feelings for him.

"I'm glad to hear that. We travel well together, don't we?" he said with a half smile. A warning smile.

"Yes. Yes, of course. Most of the time. But—but the readers of your book would—would miss you, too. And future readers of your romance will—"

"No," he replied calmly. "I may finish that romance some day, though I don't think it will be easy, but I have to write another book first. I have to address the issues that caused today's escapade."

Tabitha swallowed. "You mean, the loss of a loved one, whether from death or divorce?"

"Yeah. Too many people in this world are in pain and don't know how to recover. They strike out in pain, as Daniel did, as Curtis tried today. All they do is spread the hurt around to more people."

"And you know all about that pain, don't you, Alex?" she said in a whisper.

He looked at her sharply and then trained his gaze on his empty plate. "Yes, I do."

"If you write that book, will you be able to heal

yourself?" Tabitha held her breath, but she already knew he wouldn't ever be over Jenny.

"No, I doubt it, Tabitha." He paused, his head down. Finally he looked up. "You have to know that, Tabitha. Jenny will be the only woman for me."

"Because you don't deserve happiness?" She was pressing him, but she couldn't seem to help herself.

"Because that's my role in life. I can help people. Do you deny that?"

"No. I can't deny that. You were terrific today with Curtis and Daniel. But that doesn't mean that you can't rejoin the human race, as you put it."

"I've already done that."

"Have you? Have you dated? Kissed a woman? Had sex? Those are normal functions of a human, aren't they?"

"Are you offering, Tabitha? Is that what this is about? Your sex life? You'll have to find someone else, honey. I don't do stand-ins!"

Okay, so she'd gotten a reaction. But not the one she wanted. She stared at him, unable to hold back the tears.

"Damn! I'm sorry, Tabitha. I didn't mean to hurt you. But you have to understand. I can't do this."

Then, for the second time, he abandoned her in a restaurant.

Chapter Seven

Now what was she going to do? They still had several weeks together. He'd made it clear they could be friends but no more. Now *she* was the problem.

Tabitha tossed and turned in her bed that night. How crazy had she become? She knew he loved Jenny and always would. She had to convince him her only concern was as a friend. A friend who only offered friendship.

It would be better that way. She had fallen for the wrong guy before. Look at Derek. And Roger and Tom. Maybe she needed to forget men, to find fulfillment in her work and in her family and friends. Not in romance. Two out of three was considered good luck.

Her two sisters were happily married. Maybe she was destined to be alone…with a few good friends.

Otherwise, the tour would be an interminable hell.

Halfway through the night, she got up and composed a letter, hoping to right the wrong. Then she dressed and hurried to the door of Alex's room. She slid the paper under the door and rushed back to bed. There weren't many hours left in the night, but she hoped she could finally fall asleep.

Dear Alex,
I apologize for my remarks at dinner last night. They were out of line. But I was not offering sex. I was offering friendship. I would miss you if you were gone, and I want you to be happy.

I think your book sounds like a good idea. You have the ability to help others. Not to use that gift would be wrong.

I hope we can continue as friends, but if you feel uncomfortable, I can request that Mona find another person to accompany you.

Tabitha

Alex read through the letter twice. He'd had a sleepless night, and unfortunately, in the late hours, he'd discovered feelings for Tabitha that he felt had no place in his mind. He'd done his best to root them out.

But now she wanted friendship.

Could he manage to be friends with Tabitha and not cross the line? He had to.

Dressing for the gym, he picked up the phone and called Tabitha's room. She sounded groggy, not like her usual self. "Tabitha? Are you all right?"

"I'm fine. I overslept."

"I was going to go work out before breakfast. Want to join me?"

"No, not this morning. I—I'll meet you in the coffee shop for breakfast in an hour."

"Okay," Alex said. Then, after drawing a deep breath, he said, "I appreciated your letter. I don't see any need to make a change now. Do you?"

"No, of course not, as long as you're okay," she said slowly.

"Yeah. I'll see you at breakfast." And he hung up the phone.

It was the first day on the entire tour that she hadn't worked out. He frowned, knowing that meant she was still worried about the tour. But he vowed to himself he wouldn't be the problem. He'd settled everything in his mind. If friendship was what she wanted, friendship was what she'd get.

He was five minutes early to breakfast, anxiously waiting for Tabitha. When he saw her get out of the elevator, he breathed a sigh of relief.

"How are you feeling?" he asked at once.

"A little sluggish. I missed working out."

"I missed you being there. I like the companionship."

She smiled, but it wasn't the brightest smile he'd ever seen.

"We can work out tonight when we come back for dinner. Two workouts a day won't hurt me." He waited anxiously for her response.

"You wouldn't have to join me."

He stared at her, trying to read her feelings, but she showed nothing.

"We'll see how I feel then. We've got a busy day ahead of us." He knew they had a radio interview and two signings.

"Yes, of course." She ate her breakfast and paid the bill. "Ready?"

He nodded. He shouldn't expect too much. At least she was willing to continue the tour with him. It would be unsettling to change publicists now, he told himself. He and Tabitha would manage just fine.

A week later, they landed in New York City.

"Shouldn't this be the end of the tour?" Alex asked wearily as they got off the plane.

"Ordinarily, but Mona wanted you to have full exposure. We still have Philadelphia, Washington D.C., Charlotte, Miami and Atlanta. Then we go home."

"Right," Alex said, straightening his shoulders and carrying his laptop through the airport, trying to look energetic.

"We don't have anything scheduled this evening, so we can have a leisurely dinner. Or we can take in a Broadway musical if you want. Or I mean, you can. You may have friends here, or…or something."

"No, no friends. You like Broadway musicals?"

"Yes. They always seem so…so happy, so courageous. Facing the world with a song."

He grabbed their luggage off the carousel. Then, following her, they got in a taxi. "I think we should find a musical for tonight. I could use some cheery music. How about it?"

"I'd enjoy it," she said with a soft smile.

The Silhouette Reader Service™ — Here's how it works:

Accepting your 2 free books and gift places you under no obligation to buy anything. You may keep the books and gift and return the shipping statement marked "cancel." If you do not cancel, about a month later we'll send you 4 additional books and bill you just $3.57 each in the U.S., or $4.05 each in Canada, plus 25¢ shipping & handling per book and applicable taxes if any.* That's the complete price and — compared to cover prices of $4.25 each in the U.S. and $4.99 each in Canada — it's quite a bargain! You may cancel at any time, but if you choose to continue, every month we'll send you 4 more books, which you may either purchase at the discount price or return to us and cancel your subscription.

*Terms and prices subject to change without notice. Sales tax applicable in N.Y. Canadian residents will be charged applicable provincial taxes and GST.

If offer card is missing write to: Silhouette Reader Service, 3010 Walden Ave., P.O. Box 1867, Buffalo NY 14240-1867

NO POSTAGE
NECESSARY
IF MAILED
IN THE
UNITED STATES

BUSINESS REPLY MAIL

FIRST-CLASS MAIL   PERMIT NO. 717-003   BUFFALO, NY

POSTAGE WILL BE PAID BY ADDRESSEE

SILHOUETTE READER SERVICE
3010 WALDEN AVE
PO BOX 1867
BUFFALO NY 14240-9952

Do You Have the LUCKY KEY?

PLAY THE Lucky Key Game

and you can get

FREE BOOKS and a FREE GIFT!

Scratch the gold areas with a coin. Then check below to see the books and gift you can get!

YES! I have scratched off the gold areas. Please send me the 2 FREE BOOKS and GIFT for which I qualify. I understand I am under no obligation to purchase any books, as explained on the back of this card.

DETACH AND MAIL CARD TODAY!

(S-R-10/05)

310 SDL D7YZ   210 SDL D7YF

FIRST NAME   LAST NAME

ADDRESS

APT.#   CITY

STATE/ PROV.   ZIP/ POSTAL CODE

2 free books plus a free gift   1 free book

2 free books   Try Again!

www.eHarlequin.com

He hadn't found many smiles since Detroit. "Good. When we get to the hotel, I'll check with the concierge and see what we can get tickets for."

"I can do that."

"Nope. You get a night off from making my arrangements. Today, I'll make yours."

Tabitha reached her room at four and quickly unpacked. She had a black dress that would be perfect for a night at the theater, a halter dress with a flared skirt. She ran bath water, adding bubbles, a luxury she seldom took the time for.

After a lengthy bubble bath, she felt refreshed. She picked up her dress, holding it against her. Because this dress always made her feel pretty, she usually saved it for a special date. But this wasn't a date!

She flung the dress down on the bed as if it had bitten her. What was she doing? Falling back into the trap of thinking of Alex in a romantic sense? No, that would be a disaster!

"I'm…I'm just glad to be going out to see a Broadway musical," she said out loud, trying to convince herself.

The phone rang.

When she answered it, Alex spoke. "I've gotten us two tickets for the Billy Joel musical. The concierge said it had the best music. If you want, we can order some appetizers to eat before we go and then have a late supper after the show."

"That sounds wonderful! I mean, because I love a Broadway show."

"Of course."

"I'll order something for here for six-thirty. That will give us plenty of time to relax and still get to the show on time."

"Perfect. I'll see you at six-thirty."

She hung up the phone but kept her hand on it, as if unwilling to break contact with Alex. He must have the sexiest voice in the world.

That thought threw her off again. She had to stop thinking that way about him. He was unavailable. Why borrow unwanted heartbreak?

She looked for something to read to take her mind off Alex. When she could find nothing but a romance novel, which wouldn't help, she gave herself a manicure.

Then she studied the room-service menu, choosing some appetizers for them. By that time, she had to dress and then tidy the room. There was a small conversation area with a coffee table. They could sit there, each in a different chair, separated. In the theater, they'd have to sit close to each other…in the dark.

Chills traveled up her spine. She was going crazy! Alex was the center of her life right now because he was her job. She'd probably hate him once they got back to Fort Worth.

When he knocked on her door, Tabitha was cool. Until she opened the door.

"Come in, Alex. The appetizers just arrived."

"Good. The concierge said we should leave for the theater a little after seven if we want to make the first curtain."

"Oh, yes. I don't want to miss anything."

"When's the last time you were in New York?" he asked as he sat down.

"My sisters and I came after our first year of teaching."

"You're all teachers?" he asked in surprise. Then he said, "I don't know why that should surprise me. You probably have a lot in common."

Tabitha laughed at that understatement. "My sisters have both quit teaching. After the first year, Tommie realized it wasn't what she wanted. She began working in real estate, and she's very good at it. Since Teresa had her twin boys, she stays busy, but she's working on another children's story."

"Does she do her own illustrations?" Alex asked, watching her curiously.

"Yes, she's the artistic one."

"And Tommie is the..."

"Ambitious one."

"What are you?" he asked.

With a sigh, Tabitha leaned forward and picked up a piece of cheese. "I don't know. I don't think I've found my talent yet."

"You're terrific at what you're doing now."

She gave him a quick smile but shrugged dismissively.

"I'm serious, Tabitha. You've been terrific even when things didn't go as planned," he added. "Or maybe I should say *especially* when things didn't go as planned."

"I'm glad you think so, Alex. I may ask you for a reference." That was, if she decided on a career change, or on doing some publicity work in the summers.

"You've got it. Though I doubt Mona will need proof. You're still sending her tapes, aren't you?"

Tabitha blushed. "Most of them. I'll admit that I

skipped that one in St. Paul where your interviewer went to sleep."

Alex chuckled. "Yeah, that didn't do much for my self-esteem. But I don't think the viewing audience could tell since they kept the camera on me while they woke him up."

"It wasn't your fault," Tabitha protested.

"I hope not." Alex looked down at his watch. "We'd better leave soon so we make the show."

"Let me get my wrap."

"You know," he said as he stood, "if you dressed like that when we went for interviews, I don't think any man would fall asleep."

Her head snapped up at his compliment. "Thank you…I think."

Reaching out for her wrap, he put it around her shoulders, his touch evident through the thin material. "That shouldn't surprise you, Tabitha. You've looked in a mirror before. And you have two sisters who look just like you."

"I was surprised because you don't make it a habit to compliment me." Like never, she thought.

"Time to go," he said, heading for the door as if she hadn't spoken.

Of course not. She'd crossed that forbidden line. She'd gotten personal. She promised herself she wouldn't make that mistake again.

After the show, Alex took her to an intimate little restaurant he said he'd visited a few times. Tabitha loved it. They sat at a cozy table for two in an out-of-the-way corner and discussed the show. They'd both enjoyed the music. Even Alex couldn't help humming the songs.

"You were right, Tabitha. I feel much better after that show. The music keeps running through my mind."

"Me, too. Stop me if I break out in a chorus!"

"I don't know. I might enjoy that. Would you dance on my table?"

"Absolutely not." Their laughter was cut short by a booming voice.

"Alexander."

Both Alex and Tabitha looked up at the man standing by their table, frowning. Then Alex stood. "Father."

"I didn't know you were in town."

Tabitha stared at the man; he looked a great deal like his son, but there was no twinkle in his eye, no pleasure at seeing his son unexpectedly.

"I'm doing a book tour," Alex said but offered no apology for not informing his father of his visit.

"Will you introduce me to Jennifer?"

Tabitha gasped, but Alex didn't appear fazed.

"May I present my publicist, Tabitha Tyler."

"I beg your pardon, Miss Tyler. I thought you were Alexander's wife, Jennifer."

"That's quite all right," Tabitha lied. How could a father be so much outside his son's life? She knew her mother wouldn't stand for such distance. But then, her mother had never looked at her as if she were an interesting specimen.

Alex didn't invite his father to join them. Nor did he sit down. He just stood there, as if waiting for his father to make a move.

"Your mother is here," Mr. Myerson said.

"Is she? How nice."

Tabitha blinked at the cold-blooded conversation.

"Tell her I said hello," Alex added.

The man nodded and turned and walked away.

Tabitha stared after him, until he sat down at a table for two where a woman sat stiffly. Alex's mother was fifteen feet away and she didn't get up and come hug her son, or even speak to him?

"I apologize, Tabitha. It didn't occur to me that they would be in town, or I would've chosen another restaurant."

Snapping her gaze back to her companion, Tabitha swallowed and then said, "They come here a lot?"

"Yeah, it belongs to a friend of theirs. But the food is good."

"They live here in the city?"

"No, they live upstate."

The waiter arrived with their food, and after he left the table, Alex smiled at her and picked up his fork. "You're going to love the chicken alfredo. It's great."

"That's all you've got to say?"

"You want me to tell you how they prepared it?" he asked, raising one eyebrow as if he were doing his best to charm her.

Tabitha felt a headache developing and rubbed her forehead. "Aren't you going to go speak to your mother?"

"No."

"Why? And why doesn't she come over here?"

"Honey, you may have a warm, close family, but believe me, that's the rarity in society today." He paused, then added, "Eat your dinner."

She automatically picked up her fork, but she couldn't quite take a bite. She looked over at the other table and saw the woman staring at them. "She's looking at us."

"Can't arrest her for that," Alex said, as if it didn't matter.

"When's the last time you saw your parents?"

"About five years ago. Before I met Jenny."

"They never met your wife? And they don't know she's dead?"

Alex stared at her. "This is none of your business, Tabitha. Eat your dinner."

Tabitha silently recited her mantra. "Don't get personal." But it was difficult to concentrate on her food with Alex's parents staring at them.

When she'd eaten about half of her meal, she put down her fork. "I'm not hungry anymore. But the food was certainly delicious."

Another man, wearing a white shirt and apron and a chef's hat, paused by the table. "I'm delighted to hear your opinion, young lady. Alex, your companion is a woman of good taste!"

"Of course, Mario. Just like me." He stood and embraced the man in a bear hug, showing a warmth that had been absent with his father.

"Good to see you, boy. Are you all right?"

"I'm fine. They aren't heathens in Fort Worth, I promise." Alex shot an apologetic smile toward Tabitha.

"Aren't you going to introduce me to the lady?" Mario asked.

"Sure. Tabitha, this is the chef, Mario Andicetti, and Mario, this is my publicist, Tabitha Tyler."

"Publicist? What do you need a publicist for?"

"I'm doing a publicity tour for a book I wrote."

"You wrote a book? That's wonderful, Alex!" the man said, immediately hugging Alex again. "I always said you were a good boy. I'll go out and buy it at once."

"No, Mario, I'll bring you a copy."

"Will you autograph it?"

"Sure, just for you," Alex said with a grin.

"When? When will you bring it by?"

Tabitha could see Alex didn't have a ready answer. "We could bring it by in the morning about eleven, after we finish an interview. Would that be all right?" she asked.

"Perfect. And I'll fix you lunch. We'll celebrate!"

"Mario, you don't have to—" Alex began.

"Yes, yes, yes!" Then Mario looked at Tabitha. "You'll bring him?"

"Yes, of course." Tabitha avoided looking at Alex. She wasn't sure he would approve of her cooperation.

"This lady is nice, Alex," Mario said with twinkling eyes.

Tabitha almost wanted to cover his mouth with her hand to stop what he was saying. She knew how Alex would react.

But instead of withdrawing, Alex smiled at Mario and agreed. "Yes, she is. She's doing a wonderful job as my publicist." He emphasized that last word, as if sending a message.

"Good. I will see you both tomorrow."

Mario moved across the room, greeting other diners.

Tabitha noted that he stopped at Alex's parents' table, but the couple exuded no enthusiasm to match Mario's.

"What a lovely man," Tabitha said. She could still feel the warmth from his personality.

"Yeah, Mario is great. I even waited tables here one summer while I was in college. He's wonderful, but he's a stern taskmaster, too."

"I can imagine. Were you a good waiter?"

"One of his best," Alex said without blushing. "But I shouldn't have brought you here."

"Because of your parents?"

"Not really, because I didn't know they were in town. But because of Mario. He makes everything personal, and we've sort of agreed to stay away from personal things. My mistake."

She set out to reassure him. "Really, I don't mind, Alex."

"Thanks, but I do."

Chapter Eight

Tabitha carefully kept her distance in the taxi to the hotel. Again, Alex had made himself clear. There was nothing personal between them.

When they entered the elevator to go up to their rooms, Alex smiled at her. "I enjoyed the musical this evening. That was a good suggestion."

"I'm glad you liked it," she said, not looking at him.

"Tabitha, I didn't mean to hurt your feelings. I just didn't want to—"

"Get personal. Yes, I got that, Alex."

"I was going to say I didn't want to involve you with my family," he muttered, getting off the elevator on her floor.

"What are you doing? Your room is two floors up."

"It's late at night. I want to be sure you get to your room all right."

"I'm fine. Don't let me keep you." At this point she'd prefer a stalker to him.

Silently, he followed her to her room. Then, when she unlocked her door, he followed her in.

Before she could question why, she noticed the blinking light on her phone. "I've got a message."

"Now? Could it be Mona?"

"Tommie!" Tabitha gasped and ran for the phone. The message, as she'd expected, was about the birth of Tommie's little girl. Teresa gave all the essential information in the message but asked Tabitha to call.

"My sister had her baby. I've got to call."

It never occurred to her that Alex would remain in her room. She didn't have time to even think about him. "Teresa? Is it too late to call?"

"No, I was waiting up to hear from you. I'd begun to worry."

"Oh, we went to a musical and dinner afterward."

"We? Who is we?"

"That doesn't matter!" Tabitha protested. "Tell me about Tommie and the baby. Is everything all right?"

"Oh, yes, they're both fine. In fact, we took pictures with our digital camera so we could send them to your hotel, but I wanted to wait until you called."

She turned to Alex. "Will they let my sister send digital pictures here to the hotel?"

"I'm sure they would, but why not have her send them to my laptop?"

"Do you mind?"

"Not at all." He gave her his e-mail address, which she passed on to Teresa.

Alex stood. "I'll go get my laptop. You'll be able to see them in a couple of minutes." He left the room.

"Alex has gone to get his computer," she explained to Teresa.

"He doesn't keep it in the same room as you?"

"Teresa, of course not!"

"Well, you were out on a date. I thought—"

"We weren't on a date! We just took the night off. But we don't—don't get personal with each other."

"Why not?" Teresa asked as Alex came back into the room.

He sat down on the bed beside her and opened up his laptop. He clicked a few keys and turned the computer toward Tabitha. "Here's your niece."

Tabitha gasped as the first image of a sleeping baby, wrapped tightly in a pink blanket, came into view.

"Oh, look! Isn't she beautiful?" Tabitha whispered, tears in her eyes. "Teresa, I can see her. She's wonderful. Tell Tommie I love her and I wish I was there."

"She knows, honey, she knows. She was more worried about you feeling left out than she was about how long she was in labor."

"Did it last long?"

"Not the intense part. She was in labor for about nine hours, but the hard part went fast."

"Thank you so much for sending the picture."

"Pictures, Tab. There are six of them."

"Okay, I'll look at them. Bye."

Tabitha looked at Alex. "There are six pictures."

"Yeah, I know. I was waiting until you finished talking. Ready for the next one?"

"Yes." Together they huddled on the bed with the computer between them. The next picture showed Tommie holding her baby.

"Hey, you do look just like your sister, don't you?" Alex said, staring at the photo.

Tabitha nodded.

"Ready for the next one?"

After she said yes, Alex clicked for the next picture. This photo showed Pete and Tommie, Teresa and Jim with the baby.

"I forgot to ask what she named her," Tabitha said, reaching for the phone again.

"Don't you think it's too late?" Alex asked. He didn't look up from the picture.

"Maybe you're right. I'll call in the morning."

She waited for him to draw up the next picture, but he was still looking at the two couples on the screen. "Alex?"

"What?"

"Can I see the next one?"

"Yeah, sure. I was just thinking that since your brothers-in-law look a lot alike too, Jim knows what his baby girl will look like if they have one."

"I guess so," Tabitha said, waiting for the next picture. *Click.* The photo showed a smiling Tommie with an unwrapped baby, her hands and feet wiggling.

"Oh, look! Isn't she darling?"

"Yes, she is. But why are you crying?"

Tabitha looked up in surprise. Then she wiped her cheeks with her hands. "I don't know…I'm just so happy."

"Okay, let's see the next picture."

"Oh, that's Mom and Joel with Tommie and the baby."

"Your mother's not as blond as the three of you."

"No. Our dad had real light hair. At least, in the pictures. I never met him."

"Why not?"

"He was killed before we were born. Mom named Tommie Thomasina after Dad, who was named Thomas, because none of us was a boy."

"And who's Joel?" Alex asked, pointing to the man with her mother.

"That's Mom's husband. They married several months ago. He's wonderful, and Mom's very happy."

"Okay, last one." Alex clicked the mouse and another picture came into view. It was Pete and Tommie, with the baby, Jim and Teresa, Ann and Joel, and another lady.

"Who's this?" Alex asked.

"That's Evelyn, Jim and Pete's mom. She's part of the family now, too."

"You're not kin to her."

"Of course not, but Teresa and Tommie are. It's a kind of honorary kinship. She doesn't have anyone else, so it would be rude to leave her out."

"Clearly your family is different from mine. It's rude to *include* anyone in my family."

"Can I go through the pictures one more time?" Tabitha asked, her eyes shining with unshed tears.

"Sure," Alex agreed and wrapped his arm around Tabitha's shoulders. She leaned her head against his shoulder as he showed her the pictures one more time.

* * *

When Tabitha looked up at Alex, a smile of excitement on her lips and more tears in her eyes, he couldn't help himself. He lowered his lips to hers and pulled her closer to him. For the first time since he'd met her, he gave in to the attraction he'd felt all along.

Suddenly Tabitha jerked out of his embrace. "Get out!" she screamed, pointing to the door in melodramatic fashion.

"But, Tabitha, I—"

"No! I can't stand this yo-yo existence. I can accept 'nothing personal,' but you've got to stick to that rule, too. So don't tell me in the morning you want a change of publicist. I've obeyed your rules. Now you have to obey mine!"

Alex stared at her. Okay, he'd given in to the moment, but he hadn't meant… With Tabitha staring at him, her jaw firm, her finger pointing to the door, he didn't feel he had a choice. And he needed time to think about that kiss.

"I apologize," he began, but Tabitha was having none of it.

"Just go!" she snapped.

He took his laptop and left the room. As he rode up in the elevator to his floor, he kept thinking about how right it had felt to take Tabitha in his arms. Her lips had been soft and tremulous and had clung to his—until she'd changed her mind.

Not that he could blame her. He'd been lost in a fog of bereavement when he'd met her. She'd been his guide, leading him back to normalcy, even if she hadn't realized it.

Had he woken up too late? Had he pushed Tabitha away one too many times? He hoped not.

"So what do I do now?" he asked himself as he lay on his lonely bed. He was a gentleman, that much he was sure of. And as such, he could never ask Tabitha to leave. She was trapped in his company as publicist until they reached home.

Then he could court her, he realized. Then he could try to persuade her that he had feelings for her. That he loved her.

Because he did. It didn't mean he didn't love Jenny, because he always would. But Jenny was in his past. And he wanted a future. With Tabitha. The whole enchilada. Babies, grandbabies, family. Something he'd never known.

Tabitha had spent a restless night, but she was determined not to let it, or her feelings for Alex, show the next morning. Not only did she need to remain distant to complete the tour, but she also needed to remember that she frequently made mistakes in romance. While her sisters had found true love, she hadn't. And she didn't trust herself to make the right decision while she was away from home. She needed her sisters to help ground her.

She met Alex in the lobby for their taxi ride to another talk show. And she reminded him they would go to Mario's restaurant for lunch with a copy of his book.

"I have it here," Alex assured her with a smile.

She hurriedly looked away. "Good." Then she began going over the particulars of the interview, hoping to keep all the conversation on business.

"Did you call Teresa this morning?"

"Yes."

"What did they name the baby?"

"Marisa Ann," Tabitha said, working hard to keep her voice impersonal.

"What's the last name?" he asked.

She snapped her head around to stare at him. "Why?"

"To see if Marisa Ann goes with the last name."

"Schofield. It goes just fine with that. And Ann is my mother's name."

"You're right. Marisa Ann Schofield. I like it."

"I'll be sure to tell Tommie you approve," she said with a snippy air and turned away from him.

He deserved it. His courtship of Tabitha might be difficult, but it would also be joyous. When he could begin. This blasted tour seemed to go on forever.

After the interview, they caught another taxi and headed for Mario's restaurant.

"Are you sure we should eat lunch there?" she asked, having second thoughts. "He wouldn't let me pay last night, and—"

"He'll be hurt if we don't. He's always been my family. He's the one who hugs me, welcomes me. You saw my parents last night. You can see they're not the demonstrative kind."

"Definitely," she said in a low voice.

Alex sighed. "I know. That's why I try to keep them out of my life. It's embarrassing that my parents don't love me."

"It's not your fault. There's something wrong with them, not you."

Her strong words didn't tell him anything he didn't know, but it meant a lot to hear them from her. "Thanks," he said, picking up her hand and carrying it to his lips.

She jerked it out of his hand. "No! That's not allowed."

While she stared out the window of the taxi, Alex thought about trying to inform her of his newly discovered feelings. But he knew he shouldn't. Fortunately for his self-discipline, they soon arrived at Mario's restaurant.

They got out of the taxi and walked up to the restaurant. "Look," Tabitha said. "It says it's closed for a private party. Should we go somewhere else?"

"No, honey, we're the private party," Alex assured her, reaching past her to push open the door of the restaurant.

Mario's voice boomed out at once. "Alex! Come in. We've been waiting. And you too, Tabitha, pretty lady."

Tabitha blushed as she shook Mario's hand, and Alex thought she'd never looked more beautiful.

Alex, after receiving Mario's hug, shook hands with several of his friends who still waited tables at Mario's. Then he froze as his mother and father stepped in front of him. His father offered his hand and Alex shook it, but he was suddenly uncomfortable. Tabitha appeared at his side and shook hands with his father. Then she turned to his mother.

"I don't believe I met you last night, Mrs. Myerson. I'm Tabitha Tyler, Alex's publicist." She held out her hand and the woman, seemingly reluctant, shook it.

"How do you do?" she asked politely.

"I'm enjoying the tour with Alex. He's been so well-received. His signings draw crowds, and his book is in demand all over the country."

"How nice," the woman responded, as if Tabitha had said they were having good weather today.

"Hello, Mother," Alex said politely. "I didn't realize you and Father would be here today."

"Mario thought we should be," his father said stiffly.

Tabitha squared her shoulders. She couldn't believe how his parents were treating Alex, as if he was an un- usual bug they could study. "Have you seen his book yet? It's wonderful."

"No, we haven't," his mother said, but her words held no interest.

"Come sit down," Mario called, joy in his voice. Tabitha prayed she wouldn't be placed next to Mr. or Mrs. Myerson.

She found herself at a table for twelve, fortunately seated between Mario and Alex. Mario kept up a run- ning conversation about the food he had prepared. In be- tween, he threw in remarks about Alex and his parents. Tabitha was mesmerized by Mario's conversation.

"They never intended to have a child," Mario whis- pered. Then he told her to taste the stuffed mushrooms.

She did so, assuring him they were great.

"If they hadn't hired a nanny, I'm not sure he would've survived. But they sent him away to school when he was eight." Mario reached for another dish for her to sample.

"I let him come here during the summer. He can cook really well. I thought he might become a chef." He handed her another platter. "Don't pass up the fettuccine."

Tabitha was sure she'd gain ten pounds in this one lunch, but she wouldn't have left the restaurant even if she could. She wouldn't miss hearing about Alex.

Mario continued, "After college, he opened up a practice here in the city, but it was only a few years later that he moved away. He went to Fort Worth to get away from them." Mario nodded his head toward Alex's parents. "I've missed him."

On the other side of her, Alex nudged her. "Hey, what are you two talking about?"

"The—the cuisine. I hear you're a wonderful cook."

"Yeah. Mario wanted me to become a chef. I was a great disappointment to him."

"Don't be silly, Alex. He's very proud of you."

He gave her a smile before he turned back to his friend on his right-hand side.

She turned back to Mario. "I think what you've told me is very sad."

"Yes, but he survived. He's doing very well now, isn't he?"

"Yes, Mario, he's doing well."

"Good. Ah, dessert. You must try the tiramisu."

It was clear to Tabitha that Alex would've preferred she not meet his parents, as if he thought she'd think less of him because his parents didn't seem to care about him.

Instead, she was impressed with his courage and resolution.

When they left New York, he heaved a large sigh.

"Glad New York is behind us?"

"Yes, I am. I'm sorry you had to meet my parents."
He was frowning out the window while he spoke.

"Alex, you're not responsible for your parents. I have
great admiration for you that you're so accomplished
without them being there for you."

"I had Mario," he finally muttered.

"Yes, he seems to be a great friend."

"He liked you."

As if that mattered, Tabitha thought. Nothing mattered as long as Alex could only think about Jenny.

"He's easy to talk to." She shuffled papers in her lap.
"Now, in Philadelphia, we hit the ground running.
You'll have an interview with…"

When they finished the tour in Atlanta, Tabitha got
them to the airport in plenty of time to catch their flight.
She was proud of herself. Not for having a good tour.
But for hiding her emotions, keeping her distance, as
he'd first requested.

It hadn't been easy. The man was a charmer when
he wanted to be. Even in a bad mood, he could tug on
Tabitha's heartstrings.

She'd remained firm, however, in spite of her yearn-
ings. She was not going to suffer heartbreak like her sister Teresa. And she was not going to get pregnant either.
Instead, she was concentrating on her career. She had
some decisions to make. Mona had asked her to continue working with her, flying about the country with
prospective clients.

After Alex, she could handle anything.

"I'm glad we're going home," Alex said as they waited to board the plane.

"Yes, it's been a long tour, but you've done very well. I think your publisher will be pleased."

"I should hope so. I'd hate to think I wasted all this time and effort for nothing."

Tabitha gave him a brief smile, hoping she hid her hurt feelings.

"I didn't mean anything about you, Tabitha," Alex hurriedly said. "You've been more than terrific."

"Thank you."

She had no papers left to distract him from anything personal, so she jumped to her feet. "I'm going to get a cup of coffee. May I get one for you?"

"I'll come with you," he said, standing.

"I was hoping I could leave everything here with you while I got the coffee."

"Okay, fine. I'll take a cup," he said as he sat back down.

Tabitha breathed a sigh of relief as she escaped his presence. The tour was ending none too soon.

She took her time getting the coffee. Fifteen minutes later she returned to their seats and handed a cup to Alex.

"I thought maybe you'd gotten lost. They should start boarding soon," Alex said, looking uneasily at the airline personnel behind the ticket desk.

"Is something wrong?"

"I don't know. Several official-looking men have come to the ticket desk and had a conference with the others. But then they went away and no one has said anything. I—"

"Attention those passengers waiting for Flight six-oh-one scheduled to depart in half an hour for the Dallas-Fort Worth Airport. Unfortunately, we are experiencing difficulties with the plane that has just arrived. We are looking for another plane to take its place. We hope you will be patient."

"Do we have a choice?" Alex muttered, along with many others.

"Apparently not," Tabitha returned. She didn't want to be stuck in an airport with Alex any longer than she had to be. "I think I'll walk around for a while. I get tired of sitting all day."

"Stay within earshot so if they arrange something quickly, you can get back. I don't want to leave you behind," he teased with a smile.

"No, I don't want to be left behind. I'll stay close."

Tabitha slowly strolled along the walkway, studying the windows of the shops selling any kind of souvenir or necessity imaginable. But she wasn't in the mood to shop. She wanted to go home. To get away from Alex. To see her family.

"Attention, passengers of Flight six-oh-one. We regret to inform you that this flight has been cancelled. We will try to get as many of you as possible on the next flight, leaving in an hour. Please approach the desk in an orderly fashion, and we will—"

There was no need for the gate attendant to finish because a wild stampede surged toward her.

Tabitha groaned. She would be last in line and had no chance of getting a seat, much less two, on the next flight.

Chapter Nine

Tabitha remembered her cell phone. She pulled it out of her purse and called the airline. She requested two seats on the next flight. When the attendant came back on the phone, she said she'd managed to secure one seat on the next flight and one on the flight afterwards.

Or she might be able to get two seats on the second flight.

It didn't take long for Tabitha to make her decision. "My client will take the first flight and I'll take the second one at eight o'clock."

After she had completed their business, she put away her phone and came back to Alex. "I got you a seat on the next flight," she told him.

He looked from her to the mob around the flight desk. "How did you manage that?"

"I used my cell phone to call."

"So we only have to wait an hour? Good job, Tabitha," Alex said with his charming smile.

Tabitha looked away. "No. There was just one seat. I'll follow on the second flight."

"I'll wait and fly with you," he immediately said.

"No, there's no need for that. I've already arranged the flights. It's not a problem for me."

"But I know how eager you are to get home and meet little Marisa. Wouldn't you prefer to take the first flight and let me wait for the second?"

"That's very generous of you, Alex, but we'll leave it the way it is. Now, do you want some lunch, since we have an hour before your flight leaves?"

"Sure. That's a good idea."

But the airport restaurants were so crowded, they bought some sandwiches to take back to the waiting area.

"Well, our last meal together for the tour is a little anticlimactic, isn't it?" Alex said.

"I'm sorry."

He looked at her, a frown on his brow. "I'm not complaining, Tabitha. Sharing a meal with you anywhere is always enjoyable. Here's to many more," he said, smiling and holding up his can of soda.

Tabitha clinked her diet cola against his soda can, but with less enthusiasm. "Would you do another publicity tour with your new book?" she asked.

"That'd be up to my publisher, but I hope another one won't be necessary. At least not one as long as this one." He took a bite of his sandwich.

"How's the book coming? Have you had much chance to write?"

He nodded and swallowed. "It's in a rough stage, for sure, and it needs rethinking in certain parts of the outline. But I think it has an important message."

"I'm sure it does."

"After I've finished it, would you consider reading it and giving me your opinion?"

"*Me?* I have no expertise in psychology."

"I'm not writing the book for other psychologists to read. I'm writing it for the public, to help them if they suffer a loss that almost destroys them."

Tabitha knew he was talking about his own loss, and involuntarily her heart went out to him. She bit her bottom lip to curb her emotion. She needed to keep firm in her resolve. "I suppose I could. If I'm not on tour."

"So you have decided to switch to publicity?"

"I'm going to give it a try for the rest of the summer. Though I'll keep making my exercise videos. I think that'll be about all I can handle."

"That's quite a full plate," Alex said. "Are you going to leave yourself enough time to have a social life?"

"Probably," Tabitha answered dismissively, hurriedly searching for another impersonal subject. "I think they're going to start boarding soon. Some of the people are beginning to gather. You'd better go check with the desk."

"Are you sure I shouldn't wait for you?"

"I'm sure." She left no doubt in her voice. If he took the first flight, she could relax on the second, knowing that she'd done her job. Knowing that she wouldn't be faced with that warm smile, tempted by those lips, driven crazy by his touch.

He frowned, but he took his ticket from her and got up to approach the desk. While he did so, Tabitha threw away the trash from their impromptu picnic. Then she watched anxiously to be sure he would leave on the next plane.

Still frowning, he came back to sit down.

"Is there a problem?"

"No, I'm all set. I just wanted to make sure you'll be all right here by yourself. Your plane doesn't get in until late."

"Mom and Joel will probably meet me. I'll call them after I get you off. Mona will meet you at the airport and make sure you get home."

"That's not necessary."

"She was planning on meeting both of us. I'll call and let her know about the change of plans." She took out her phone and called Mona. After that conversation, which included a promise to come to the office the next day for an evaluation of the tour and a discussion about Tabitha's future, Tabitha confirmed what she'd said earlier.

"Yes, Mona will meet you."

"But I'll be on my home turf. I think I can manage to get home alone."

"Mona will hire a car and meet you. Then she can be sure you got home safely."

"And you're meeting with her tomorrow?"

Tabitha nodded.

"Should I come in, too, to discuss the tour?"

"No, that's not necessary, but thank you for offering."

"So, when will I see you again?"

Her head jerked up and she stared at him. Then she

said, "I'm sure we'll run into each other at some time or another."

He looked solemn. "I'm being serious, Tabitha. I don't want to lose touch with you."

The call for first-class passengers saved Tabitha from answering. "Time for you to go. Have a nice flight," she said, standing.

Alex stood, gathering his belongings. Then, before Tabitha realized his intentions, he swooped down and kissed her. "I'll see you at home," he told her and headed toward the gate.

She watched him go with tears in her eyes. Damn the man! He changed the rules on her constantly. Fortunately, she didn't have to deal with him anymore.

But she would miss him. He'd been a great traveling companion, except for the days when he remembered Jenny. There had been many memorable moments on the tour that would be with her for a long time.

She sat there until the plane pulled away from the gate, fearing it might be canceled. When Alex was definitely gone, she checked on the status of her ticket. She had two hours before her flight left.

Finding a quiet corner, she called her mother. "I'm at the airport in Atlanta. I won't be arriving tonight until about ten. Could you and Joel come pick me up?"

"I'm sure we can. Let me just check with Joel," Ann said, covering the phone for a minute to check with her husband. "Yes, dear, we'll be there. Are you all right?"

"I— Yes, of course. I just miss all of you. It'll be good to see some friendly faces."

"Will we need to drop your client somewhere?"

"No, I managed to get him a seat on the flight that just left. He'll be there in an hour or so. Mona is going to take care of him."

"Good. But I'm afraid it'll be too late to go see the baby. Tommie and Pete are struggling to get enough sleep right now, since the baby eats every two or three hours."

"I didn't expect to see them tonight."

"All right, dear. We'll see you soon."

The warmth of her mother's voice soothed some of the scars of the tour. But it also made her remember Alex's parents. He'd been strong in spite of their indifference. She guessed she was the weaker of the two, since she needed her mother's support.

Especially to get over Alex.

Alex settled in his first-class seat, but he wore a frown on his face. He wished he had Tabitha next to him, as she'd been all during the tour.

A reminiscent smile replaced the frown as he remembered his first day with Tabitha. That day, he would've traded her for Mona without a thought. But not now.

He needed to finish his book. But first on his list was to reunite with Tabitha. He hadn't been able to get any kind of plans made before he'd had to leave, but he knew where to find her. At Mona's.

Besides, how many Tabitha Tylers could there be in the phone book? He'd call tonight to be sure she got home safely. Then he'd begin some casual contact, kind of sneak up on her. He had to, because he'd managed to convince Tabitha too well that he still loved Jenny.

He did and always would love Jenny, with her warmth and joie de vivre. Had she lived, he would never have left her. He wouldn't even have met Tabitha.

But she hadn't lived.

Much to his surprise, he discovered his heart had room for a beautiful blonde who drew him ever closer. Jenny was his past. Tabitha was his future.

All he had to do was convince Tabitha of that.

On her first morning home, Tabitha slept late. Well, late for her. She got up at nine and had a refreshing shower. It was a relief to be back in her own condo, with her belongings around her. Her mother and Joel had welcomed her with warm hugs last night.

Somehow, though, their welcome hadn't eased Tabitha's malaise. She fixed herself a cup of tea and some toast and had a leisurely breakfast, going through her mail. Her mother had picked it up once a week while she was gone and had kept her bills paid, so she didn't have to worry about being late.

There were some personal letters, however. Several were from women who had bought her tapes and found a different life because of their weight loss and energy level. She enjoyed those. Setting them aside to answer later, she finished her breakfast and then dressed.

It was almost eleven when she arrived at Mona's office.

"How are you?" she asked as she came in the door.

Mona, who still had casts on both legs, didn't get up. She shot Tabitha a big smile and held out her arms for a hug. "I'm getting better. And thanks to you, business is good too."

After Tabitha sat down beside her, Mona leaned forward. "I have to ask this right away because I'm dying to know. Have you decided to work for me?"

"Part of the time." At Mona's confused look, she explained, "I'd like to work with you in the summers, and I can even do a short tour during school breaks. I know I have a lot to learn, but I'm hoping you'll teach me."

"Honey, you already know a lot. Dr. Myerson couldn't stop singing your praises last night."

"We did work well together, but that was because of your wonderful plans. All I had to do was follow your directions."

"Don't worry. By your next tour, you'll be a pro." She reached out and grabbed Tabitha's hand. "I'm happy to get you at least part-time."

"It's just such a big question, Mona. I'd rather be sure."

"I understand. Now, back to Dr. Myerson. He said he was difficult early on. Did you have any problems?"

Tabitha ignored the memories that crowded into her head. "No, we made it fine."

"Great, because I've got another tour coming up. It will only be the major markets, a two-week tour. Are you up for it?"

"Of course. I need to meet my latest family member and rest a little, though. When does it start?"

"Not until a week from Monday. That gives you…ten days, I think. Long enough?"

"Yes, that'll be fine. Whom will I be escorting?"

They continued to talk business for a while. Then

Mona suggested lunch. Tabitha offered to drive, but Mona had a car on call since her accident.

"I'm paying the guy to pick me up whenever. Might as well make use of him."

Once they were in a local restaurant and had ordered, Mona looked at Tabitha. "I do need to ask you about something."

"What?" Tabitha asked.

"Last night Dr. Myerson asked for your home number. Said he wanted to call and see if you'd gotten in okay. I told him I'd check on you and let him know if there was a problem."

"Thank you," Tabitha said, shifting her gaze to her plate.

"Is there some reason he would ask that?"

"We got along well and…well, he mentioned something about wanting to keep in touch."

"So I should've given him your number?"

"No!" Tabitha drew in a deep breath. "As you know, Dr. Myerson is—is very much in love with his dead wife. I find his company a little confusing. I'm better off not to maintain the friendship."

"I know he was…" Mona said, pausing. Then she said, "He didn't mention her at all on the drive to his home. Maybe he's gotten over her."

Tabitha just shook her head and steered the conversation away from her. "He's working on another book that has grabbed his attention."

"Which reminds me," Mona said. "I haven't praised you for handling that crazy man in Detroit. I heard the station tried to hire you away from me."

"How did you know?" Tabitha asked in surprise.

"The station manager called here, looking for you. When he told me what he wanted, I told him I had first dibs," Mona looked up from her plate. "But I was kidding. If you want to go there and work in television, it's a good opportunity."

Tabitha smiled at her friend's generosity. "Thanks, Mona, but I'm not moving to Detroit. I'm a homebody. I'm staying near my family."

Mona breathed a big sigh of relief. "I can't tell you how happy I am to hear that."

Tabitha laughed. "Remember, I still haven't promised to start working for you when the summer is over. On Monday, we can start making preparations for the next tour, though."

"Great. I've already done a lot of the groundwork. You'll be seeing some of the same people. By the way, many of them called to tell me what a great job you did, too."

"That was nice of them."

"I expected to hear from Helen, too, but I didn't. Was there a problem there?"

"Helen Wilson in San Francisco? Is she a particular friend of yours?" Tabitha licked her suddenly dry lips in concern.

Mona's eyes narrowed, but she only said, "No, just an acquaintance. But she's on the list for the next tour."

"Thank God the author is a woman," Tabitha said.

"Yes, but why does that make a difference?"

Shrugging her shoulders, Tabitha said, "Helen is a widow, and when she discovered Alex had also lost his mate, she made a play for him. He panicked and insisted I join them for dinner without checking with Helen.

"I tried to make her believe I was joining them because she did such a good interview. We picked up the check, too. But Alex wanted to make sure she didn't have any lingering ideas, and he…well, he flirted with me to convince her."

"Hmm, well, I'd guess you had no choice. After all, your first allegiance is to your client. And he sounded completely satisfied. Maybe you can be extra nice to Helen on the next trip."

"Yes, that's a good idea. I should've sent her flowers," Tabitha said, frowning.

"That would've been a nice touch. Certainly Dr. Myerson couldn't do that."

"No. He wouldn't have given her any encouragement. But I convinced him to be honest with her so she wouldn't feel he'd misled her when the news of his wife's death came out. He wasn't prepared for Helen's response."

Mona reached over and patted Tabitha's hand. "Not to worry. You did a great job."

Alex stared at the telephone directory. There were no Tabitha Tylers in the phone directory. Not one. He checked the Tylers with initials. He'd heard some women listed themselves like that to avoid crank calls. No Tyler with initial T. Anywhere.

What was going on?

Okay, so he'd have to call Mona. Last night, when he'd asked for Tabitha's number, Mona had looked at him strangely. Then she'd found an excuse not to give it to him. That was why he'd put off calling her today.

But it was two o'clock.

He picked up the phone. When Mona answered, he greeted her warmly. "I just wanted to thank you for taking me home last night. I appreciated the effort."

"No problem, Dr. Myerson."

"Don't you think, since I'm calling you Mona, you should call me Alex? Tabitha does."

"Of course. I'll be delighted to call you Alex. By the way, may I use your name as a reference for my agency?"

"Absolutely, Mona. I'm a satisfied customer."

"I'm glad to hear that, Alex."

"Um, may I speak to Tabitha?"

"I'm sorry, Alex, she's already gone for the day. She should be in on Monday. I'll have her call you then, if that's all right. I'd like her to have a few days without worrying about anything business-wise."

"I'm not going to worry her. I just wanted to check in with her, see if she's doing all right." He held his breath waiting to hear if he'd convinced her.

"I haven't asked her about giving out her number. I'll have her call you Monday. Will you be home then?"

"Yeah, I'll be home," he muttered and hung up the phone.

Now what?

What else did he know about Tabitha that would help him find her? *Schofield*. He knew her brothers-in-law were Pete and Jim Schofield.

He turned back to the directory. Schofield. He found

a James Schofield, at a CPA office. Picking up the phone, he dialed the number.

"CPA Associates," a woman said in a professional voice.

"Jim Schofield, please," Alex said calmly.

"I'm sorry, but Mr. Schofield is working from home today. Can I take a message?"

"Could you give him my number and have him call me. Tell him it's about Tabitha."

"All right. What is your name and telephone number?"

After he gave her the information, he asked, "Can you call him right away?"

"Yes, sir. I'll call him right away."

His phone rang a couple of minutes later and he grabbed it at once. A deep voice asked, "Is Dr. Myerson there?"

"Yes, I'm Dr. Myerson. Is this Mr. Schofield?"

"Yes. You asked me to call?"

"Yes, I was the author on tour with Tabitha. I didn't think to ask for her number before we parted. I want to call her and see that she got home all right. Could you give me her number?"

"Hmm, I don't think I can give you her number without my wife's okay."

"Is she there?"

"No, but she should be back in a little while. I could—"

"Could I come wait for her return?"

Something in his voice must've alerted Jim. "You can't wait? She's not going anywhere."

"I want to see her."

"Maybe you'd better come over here," Jim said slowly. "I think we need to meet."

Alex didn't ask why. As soon as he hung up the phone, he got out a city map to find the street address he'd been given. It'd be good to meet Tabitha's brother-in-law. The guy would know Alex wasn't a crazy stalker but a respectable professional who wanted to see Tabitha.

Tabitha hurried to Tommie's house after lunch with Mona. It was time she met Marisa Ann, Pete and Tommie's baby girl. When she rang the doorbell, it took Tommie a few minutes to come to the door, and Tabitha hoped she hadn't woken her up.

"Tabitha! Come in!" Tommie exclaimed, opening her arms wide to her sister.

Tabitha hugged her. "I hope you weren't asleep."

"Not yet. I'm going to take a nap in a little while. Have you had lunch?"

"Yes, Mona took me to lunch."

"I want to hear all about your trip. But wait, I promised Teresa I'd call her as soon as you got here. She wants to hear too."

"Good. Tell her to bring the boys, too."

"Oh, no. We're having sister time."

"But —"

"Don't worry. We're all having dinner here tonight and the three babies will be here."

"Okay. Can I take a peek at Marisa while you call Teresa?"

"Of course. Go on up."

Tabitha ran up the stairs, anxious to meet her new

niece. Tiptoeing into the room, she stood beside the crib, staring down at the little baby wrapped in her blanket—pink, of course—her silky lashes resting on a rosy cheek. Tabitha's heart melted at once.

"Oh, you sweet baby," she whispered, fighting the urge to touch her. Maybe tonight Tommie would let her hold her.

She heard Tommie softly call her name and she returned downstairs. "Marisa is wonderful!"

"I know," Tommie said with a big smile. "I try to sound modest, but I can't. She *is* wonderful."

They hugged again. Then they strolled into the family room.

"Sit down while I put on some coffee. And I have some great cheesecake. I think you've lost weight, so you get the biggest piece."

"I haven't lost weight!" Tabitha protested. Then she relented. "Maybe…maybe a little bit. Traveling is hard work."

A knock at the front door signaled Teresa's arrival from her home only a few streets over.

"I'll go let Teresa in," Tabitha said, jumping up and going to the front door before Tommie could stop her.

"Teresa!" she exclaimed and hugged her other sister. "I'm so glad you came over. But you didn't bring the boys?"

"Nope. It's sister time. You'll see the twins tonight. How are you?"

"I'm fine. Come on, Tommie's in the kitchen."

"Does that mean cheesecake?"

"What? Do you two have a thing about cheesecake?"

"She promised to supply the cheesecake when I reached my old weight."

Tabitha took a look at her sister. "Well, you sure look good. How did you do it?"

"I used a certain person's videotapes. They're terrific," Teresa said with a grin.

Tabitha smiled in return. "Good. I'm glad you got some use out of them."

They reached the kitchen where Tommie had coffee and cake waiting. Tabitha sat down with a sigh, glad to be with her sisters again.

"Now," Tommie said calmly, "tell us about Alex and what's going on between the two of you."

Chapter Ten

Excitement rose in Alex when he parked in front of a one-story home nestled in lush foliage with several trees providing shade, something important in a Texas summer.

It was a nice home. A pricey home. But not flashy. It was what he would've expected from Tabitha's family. He drew a deep breath. Man, he hoped he wasn't making a mistake.

He got out of the car and approached the front door. After he rang the doorbell, he stood preparing a speech to convince Teresa that she should give him Tabitha's number.

When the door opened, he was taken aback to see a man standing there, a cloth diaper slung over his shoulder.

Alex couldn't think of what to say.

"Yes?" the man asked. "If you're selling something, I'm not buying."

"No! No, I'm Alex Myerson, the psychologist Tabitha Tyler took around on the publicity tour."

"Oh, yeah, hi." Jim intended to shake his hand, but a baby's scream distracted him.

"Rats! Come in. I've got to check on—"

He didn't finish the sentence since another scream, sounding the same, joined in. He headed down the hallway.

Alex stepped into the foyer, feeling guilty about invading a family moment. But he wasn't going to wait on the doorstep. He closed the door behind him.

"Do you mind coming back here?" Jim called.

Alex followed the sound of his voice and discovered him in a nursery.

"I was getting ready to give the boys their baths before I fed them and put them down for a nap. Can we talk while I work?"

"Yes, of course. First, I want to apologize for interrupting. It's kind of you to let me come right over."

Jim stared at him until one of the babies cried out again. Picking up the baby, he lowered him into a plastic tub on the top of a table. As the other baby continued to cry, Jim nodded in his direction. "You mind picking up Tommy? He'll stop crying and we can talk."

Alex wanted to talk. But pick up the baby? He'd never held a baby in his life. Slowly, he approached the crib and looked at the baby. He was waving his arms and legs frantically.

Gently, Alex slid his hand under the little boy, remembering hearing that he should support the head. The baby responded to his touch, growing silent as Alex brought him to his shoulder.

Jim was trying to bathe the other twin while he kept an eye on Alex and Tommy. "You're not used to babies?"

"No. Am I doing it right?"

Jim grinned. "He stopped crying, didn't he?"

"Yes."

"Now, why didn't Tabitha give you her number?"

"I didn't think to ask her. Things got kind of jumbled at the last minute, and she sent me ahead on a different flight. So I hoped I could talk Teresa into giving it to me."

Jim gave him a sharp look. "You know Teresa?"

"No. I've never met her. But I saw both of you in pictures the night Marisa was born. Actually, I tried reaching Tabitha at the publicist's office, but Mona said she hadn't asked her about giving me her phone number. She suggested I call back on Monday when Tabitha would be in the office."

"And you didn't want to wait that long?"

Alex let out a sigh. At last, someone who understood him. "No, I didn't. You see, my wife—"

"You're married?" Jim asked abruptly, anger in his eyes. Obviously, he felt protective about his sister-in-law.

"No! No, I'm not."

"But you said your wife—"

"My wife died a year ago."

"Oh." Jim rinsed off his young son and wrapped him in a bath towel that had a hood to cover his head. "Here, I'll trade you."

Alex exchanged babies, a maneuver that scared him to death. It didn't seem to bother the babies, however.

"Get a diaper out of the diaper holder at the end of the bed and put it over him before you dry him off. Boys have a way of being unpredictable," Jim explained, grinning again. "By the way, that's Johnny."

Immediately Alex did as Jim said.

"Okay, dry him off. And be sure you get in the creases. We've got healthy babies."

"Yes, I can tell." After drying off the wiggling baby, Alex asked, "Should I fasten the diaper?"

"Yeah. You know the padded part goes in front?"

"Oh. Okay."

"With girls, it goes behind. They make boy diapers and girl diapers now."

"I didn't know."

Jim chuckled but didn't say anything else.

When Alex had Johnny diapered, Jim directed him to put the baby into a terrycloth one-piece suit. This task was even more difficult than putting on the diaper, though it didn't carry the danger of an uncovered baby boy.

Just as he finished, Jim carried the other baby to his own bed. "Would you please do the same for Tommy while I go fix their bottles? Then we can do some real talking."

"But what about this one?" Alex demanded, panic rising as Jim headed for the door.

"He's good. Just leave him lying there. They can't pull up yet. They're only four months old."

Then he was gone.

Alex stepped away from Johnny's bed over to Tommy's bed. Okay, he'd done this once. He could do it again. Drying off Tommy, with the diaper blocking any accidents, Alex began to think he'd gotten the hang of this job.

When he removed the diaper to actually put it on the little boy, he realized Tommy had already relieved himself. Alex didn't know where to put the soiled diaper, but he knew not to put it on the baby.

Grabbing another diaper, he worked quickly to get it on Tommy. "Okay, little guy. Now all I have to do is get you dressed, like your brother."

He noticed that Tommy's little suit was green while Johnny's was blue. Good thinking. That way people wouldn't confuse them.

Jim came sailing back into the room. "All finished?"

"Yeah," Alex said, smiling with pride.

"Good. Grab one and let's go to the den. We have two rockers there. Here, you'll need one of these," Jim said, grabbing a clean cloth diaper and throwing it over Alex's shoulder.

Alex picked up Tommy and followed Jim, who was carrying Johnny in one arm, to the den.

"You're, uh, pretty good with babies," Alex said once he was seated in a rocker.

"You learn fast out of desperation. Teresa needed some sleep and I thought I'd help out when we got them home from the hospital. I had no idea what I was getting into."

But he didn't look unhappy.

"Now, put the nipple in his mouth and keep the bottle tilted up a little so the milk is always filling the nipple. We don't want him to suck in air."

Alex did as he was instructed.

"Now, you want to tell me about you and Tabitha?"

Alex began the lengthy explanation that continued for more than half an hour, thanks to interminable questions from Jim.

Finally Jim said, "Man, you have really screwed up."

"I know. But I can't fix it if I can't even talk to her."

"True. Hey, it's time to burp the boys. Put Tommy on your shoulder and pat his back until he burps."

Alex did that, expecting a delicate little sound from the babies. After all, they were very small, even if they were four months old.

Instead, both boys let out loud burps that surprised him.

"Good job, guys," Jim said lovingly. "Now we put them to bed and call Pete."

Tabitha went back to her condo after a couple of hours at Tommie's. The sisters' talk session had felt good, as had all the sessions they'd had all their lives. But she hadn't expected Tommie and Teresa to pick up on her unsettled mind. And to guess that Alex was the cause.

"Silly me," she muttered.

They'd always been able to read each other easily, except when Teresa was pregnant with Jim's babies. But Tabitha hadn't tried to hide what was happening with Alex. When she'd talked to her sisters while she was on his tour, she'd apparently let little things slip into their conversations.

So she'd explained why there was nothing between her and Alex and why there could never be. He was mourning his dead wife. She certainly wasn't going to fight a ghost for Alex. She'd lose that contest, which would lead to heartache.

Eventually, they'd switched their conversation to what Tabitha was going to do about her career. She told them that after considering working with Mona full-time, she'd decided to return to school in the fall and do publicity work in the summer.

She'd also discussed her decision with her mother on their way back from the airport. Now, all she had to do was relax and enjoy the family party.

Alex would love an evening like tonight. But he'd never had that kind of family. Jenny had been an orphan, so she hadn't been able to offer that support to him either.

Frowning, she went to run a hot bubble bath for herself, trying to shut out thoughts of Alex.

After undressing, she slid into her bath, but her wayward thoughts returned to Alex. She could picture him at home involved in his next book. He wouldn't be thinking of her.

In her head, she began to list songs she wanted to use on her next exercise tape. She couldn't wait to get started on it. Alex would tell her—

"Stop!" she ordered out loud. It was ridiculous that she couldn't think of anything without it making her think of Alex.

She got out of the tub and dried off. Then she donned her underwear and went to her closet to look for something to wear. She chose a blue floral sundress. After all, tonight Marisa would meet her Aunt Tabitha and she wanted to make a good impression.

The phone rang and Tabitha picked up the receiver to hear her mother's voice.

"Joel thought we should drop by and pick you up for the evening. That way you won't be driving home alone afterward."

"That's nice of Joel, Mom, but I can make it all right."

"I know you can, sweetheart, but there have been a lot of scams played on single women drivers lately, so we'll worry less if you let us pick you up."

"All right, if that's what you want. What time shall I be ready?"

"We'll pick you up at seven-fifteen. They want us there at seven-thirty."

"I was going to go a little early to help," Tabitha said.

"There will be nothing to do. Pete is picking up dinner at our favorite barbecue place, and Teresa and Jim are bringing dessert. We don't worry about cooking for these gatherings, you know."

"It sounds good to me. I haven't had good barbecue in six weeks," Tabitha said.

She hung up the phone and continued dressing. She had about half an hour before her mother and Joel would arrive. Plenty of time.

In fact, too much time.

No! She was not going to think of Alex again.

Instead, she turned her thoughts to her sisters and how fortunate they were. They had wonderful husbands and now wonderful babies.

Tabith wanted a wonderful marriage too. But she didn't know if that was possible. She hadn't found anyone in years who stirred her as Alex did. What if she never found someone? She was being ridiculous. There had to be another man as great as Alex but unattached.

Tabitha squared her jaw. If she didn't find anyone, she'd make the most of life, living it to the fullest. And being the best aunt her niece and nephews had ever seen. One never knew what life could bring. But she wouldn't give up.

She hurriedly put on the little makeup she usually wore and curled her hair. Then she brushed it and let its golden sheen fall to her shoulders.

Checking her appearance in the full-length mirror, she slipped her feet into slender sandals, her painted toenails showing. Ready to go, she gathered her purse and keys and moved to the front room so she could watch for Ann and Joel's car.

Almost as soon as she got to the window, she saw their sedan pull in. She opened the door and waved before pulling the door to and locking it.

"Perfect timing," she announced as she slid into the back seat. "I'd just gotten ready."

"I'm glad. We didn't want to keep you waiting," Ann said.

Joel just smiled into the rearview mirror. He didn't say much, but he was agreeable to any of his wife's plans and made it clear he considered the triplets to be his children as well as Ann's.

"Joel, how are you holding up being grandpa to three babies now?" Tabitha asked, smiling.

"Aw, I don't get to hold them very often with your mom and Evelyn around."

"Well, I'm going to fight them for time. You can join me. We'll grab all the babies and not let anyone else hold them," Tabitha assured him, teasing.

"You're looking for trouble, young lady," her mother said. "Evelyn and I are very protective of our grand-babies."

"Joel and I will take good care of them. Won't we, Joel?"

"You bet. But I can't fight your mom, Tabitha. You know that."

"I know. It's okay, Joel. But I'm still going to claim my time with the babies tonight."

"You need to have your own babies," Joel said suddenly. "Evelyn wouldn't have any claims on your baby, and your mom would only have a fourth of her time to give to your baby."

"Good idea," Tabitha said, forcing a smile. "I'll have to work on that plan."

"Not like Teresa did," Ann hurriedly said. "Make sure you're married first."

"I will, Mom."

Tabitha looked out the car window, blinking rapidly to dispel the tears. She would *not* think about Alex. Definitely not!

Actually, she didn't even know him well enough to think she could marry him. Alex was more complex than that. He looked like a hunk, but it was his mind that was his most appealing attribute. His mind and his heart. The way he'd dealt with the man in Detroit, recognizing his pain, and the host's also, spoke volumes about Alex as much as it did the two men.

She might call him next week to see if he'd heard from those two since he got back. She felt sure he would have talked to them by phone.

"Tabitha?"

"Yes, Mom?" she said, instantly clearing her head of Alex.

"We're here. Aren't you going to get out?"

"Oh, yes, of course," she said hurriedly, hoping her mother would say nothing about her distraction.

"I don't see Teresa and Jim's car. We must've beat them here," Tabitha said. "I called earlier and offered to pick up the dessert, but Teresa refused."

"I'd already offered, but she said it wouldn't be a problem. Jim was working from home today, so he could help her."

"Yes, that's why she was able to come over to Tommie's this afternoon. That's very handy for Teresa."

"Yes, it is. And he's very good with the boys."

"How's Pete with Marisa?"

Ann chuckled as Joel rang the doorbell. "He's scared to death he'll do the wrong thing and hurt her. But Tommie's teaching him."

"As long as he's willing to try," Tabitha murmured as the door opened and Pete invited them in.

"Hey, you're the first to get here. Come on in. Tommie's upstairs dressing Marisa."

"Thank you, Pete," Ann said. "Do you need any help putting out the food?"

"No, thanks, Ann. I've got it under control."

"Then Tabitha and I will go see if we can help Tommie," she said with a smile and headed for the stairway, Tabitha right behind her.

Joel and Pete stared at the ladies as they climbed the stairway.

"Ann and my mother must be in a race to see who can spend the most time with Marisa before she's a month old," Pete said.

"That's the way grandmothers are," Joel said, smiling. "If they start getting in your way, say so."

"No, that's not going to happen. By the time I get tired of it, I'll need them to baby-sit so I can get my wife to myself."

The doorbell rang again and Pete pulled the door open, letting in his mother, Teresa, Jim and his nephews. "How are you all?"

"Just fine," Evelyn said, hugging Pete. "Where's Tommie and Marisa?"

"Right here," Tommie called from the top of the stairs. Ann was beside her, carrying Marisa.

Tommie hurried down. "Come on into the family room. Oh, Teresa, I swear the boys have grown in only a week. Are they sitting up yet?"

"They can if I help them," Teresa said. "I'll show you when we get settled."

"Great." Tommie led the way to the family room that connected to the kitchen. They were eating in the dining room simply because of the numbers, not because they were being formal tonight.

As per their agreement, when Ann reached the bottom of the stairs with Marisa, she transferred the baby into Tabitha's arms. Tabitha stared down at the tiny baby, her blue eyes seeming to stare straight at her.

"Isn't she beautiful?" Evelyn whispered, staring down over Tabitha's shoulder. "I didn't get to have any girls. I just think Marisa is the sweetest thing."

"Me, too, Evelyn."

Together the two women followed the others into the family room and sat on the sofa together.

Just as they'd all settled in, the doorbell rang again.

"Oh, I forgot. I asked a friend to dinner, too," Pete said as he left the room.

Tabitha scarcely heard him because she was busy talking to Marisa, watching the baby's lips move from a rosebud into what could perhaps be called a smile.

"Whom did Pete ask to join us?" Evelyn asked.

No one answered her question.

Chapter Eleven

Alex stepped into the house. "Thanks for inviting me, Pete."

"I just hope we've made the right decision. I should've prepared my wife," Pete muttered, as if talking to himself.

"Do you want me to go?" Alex asked softly. "If you think it's going to cause your marriage difficulties, I can."

"That's not necessary. Pardon my grousing. Come on in."

Alex drew a deep breath as he followed his host. That afternoon, after Pete had joined him and Jim, they'd debated their best move. In the end, Pete had decided Alex's inclusion in the evening was the best response to the situation.

When they reached the entrance to the family room, Alex's gaze immediately focused on Tabitha, sitting on the sofa, her attention on the baby in her arms. He'd never seen such a beautiful picture.

Pete cleared his throat, and everyone except Tabitha looked up. "I'd like to introduce Dr. Alex Myerson."

"Alex?" Tabitha gasped and her head shot up.

Tabitha's response drew all eyes. Alex would have preferred that he and Tabitha reunited in private, but she'd made that impossible.

"Evening, Tabitha."

"Dear, is this the man you escorted on that publicity trip?" Ann asked.

"Yes, it is, but I didn't know he knew— You didn't know Pete! You asked his last name so you could see if Marisa went well with it."

"That's true. But I met him and Jim today and—"

"How?" Tabitha snapped.

Tommie stood and slipped her arm through her husband's. "Yes, I'd be interested in the answer to that, too."

"Jim?" Teresa called softly.

Jim immediately went to his wife's side, sitting beside her and sliding his arm around her.

"When did you meet Alex?"

"This afternoon."

"But you were home with the babies."

"Uh, yeah."

"And *you* were at work," Tommie pointed out to Pete. "So how did you both meet him?"

Alex couldn't let his newfound friends take the heat for his actions. He stepped forward. "I confess. I couldn't get Tabitha's number out of Mona, and she wanted me to wait until next Monday to talk to Tabitha. But I didn't want to wait. I called Jim's office and gave them my number and asked him to call. Then I went to his house to ask Teresa to give me the number."

"He helped me bathe the boys," Jim added, "and explained his problem to me. I called Pete to come meet him and…and it seemed to us a good thing to invite him to dinner."

There was an embarrassing silence after Jim stopped talking. Alex felt he might have to leave after all. But Ann, whom he recognized from the pictures, stood and offered her hand.

"How do you do, Dr. Myerson? Welcome to our family evening."

"Thank you, Mrs.….I'm sorry, I only know you as Ann."

Joel stood and offered his hand. "That's all right. I'm Joel Anderson, her husband. But please call me Joel."

"Thank you. And please call me Alex."

"Are you a medical doctor?" Evelyn asked, still a little puzzled.

"No, ma'am, I'm a psychologist," Alex explained.

Tabitha's sisters introduced themselves after he shook hands with Evelyn.

"Tabitha told me about being a triplet, but I had difficulty wrapping my mind around three of her. All of you are so beautiful."

"Well, that's one way to make us like you," Tommie said with a laugh.

"The other," Teresa added softly, "is to be good to Tabitha."

Tabitha turned a bright red. "That's not necessary. Alex is—is a friend, that's all. We travel well together."

"We work well together, too. Remember Detroit?"

Tabitha nodded but said nothing else.

Jim frowned. "What happened in Detroit?"

"Tabitha didn't tell you?" Alex's gaze traveled back to Tabitha in surprise, but she just shrugged her shoulders.

Alex turned back to his audience. "A man interrupted my television interview."

"Oh?" Ann said. "Tabitha didn't mention that."

"Because Alex handled it well, no one was disturbed."

"Of course, you weren't in any danger," Joel said, to reassure his wife.

"She wasn't until she stepped onto the sound stage to offer a suggestion, which was brilliant," Alex said, smiling at Tabitha, wanting her family to realize how well she'd done.

"The situation was already defused by Alex before I stepped in," Tabitha said. "He talked the man to reason. Then the host began to cry and confessed his own pain from his divorce. It was a very healing interview."

"Did it get on television?" Pete asked. "We didn't see anything on it."

"No. They filled in with an earlier taped program." Alex murmured. "Of course, because Tabitha advised them to pay for grief counseling for both men and have a small segment on each show with the progress they'd made, they're going to do a lot of good for anyone dealing with loss."

"Have you talked to them?" Tabitha asked.

"Yeah, I have. I wanted to tell you that. I called the studio this morning. Everything's going well."

"Good."

"Well, now that we've settled all that," Pete said, "it's time to eat. Gentlemen, join me in preparing the feast."

Joel and Jim showed no hesitation, but Alex looked at Pete questioningly. "Me, too?"

"You bet. We do the hard part tonight. Put out the food. Come on, Alex, you get Table Setting 101 with Jim. Just follow his lead. He's been well instructed by his wife."

"Yes, sir," Alex agreed.

The women played with the babies while the men got dinner ready. Tabitha traded Marisa to Evelyn so she could play with one of the boys. She took Tommy in her lap while Ann held Johnny.

In spite of playing with the baby, Tabitha kept an eye on Alex's comings and goings. He seemed to get along well with the men of her family.

"So Alex is experienced with babies?" Teresa asked as she moved to sit beside Tabitha.

Tabitha jerked her gaze away from Alex. "Uh, no, I don't think so."

"But Jim said he helped him bathe and dress the boys."

"I'm sure Jim was teasing you. He wouldn't allow a stranger to handle the babies."

"Hmm. I think I need to do a little questioning of my husband."

"I'm sorry, Teresa. I had no idea Alex would even care that he didn't have my home number."

Tommie joined her sisters. "He seems very nice."

"He is. He's…wonderful. I mean wonderfully companionable. Most of the time." She felt her cheeks flush and wished she could hide for a few moments to gain some composure.

Teresa chuckled gently. "I guess he is. And not too hard on the eyes, either."

"And he has great manners. He seems quite comfortable among the family," Tommie said. "He must have a nice family, too."

Tabitha wanted to ignore that statement, to pretend she hadn't heard. But she'd never lied to her sisters. "He comes from a horrible family. His mother and father are stiff and cold. They have very little interest in him and don't stay in touch."

"He told you that?" Tommie asked in horror.

"No, I met them in New York City. Accidentally. They were like blocks of ice. Mario said—"

"His father's name is Mario?" Teresa asked in surprise.

"No. Mario is a friend who has a restaurant in Manhattan where we went to eat. Alex worked there in the summers as he grew up. He loves Mario like a father. But his parents were there dining and—"

"Dinner is served, ladies," Pete called out. "Collect your plate and go down the buffet. Then be seated at the dining table."

"We have to put the babies down first, Pete," Tommie reminded him.

"Oops, I forgot. We haven't had ours long enough for me to remember these things. We've got a crib for Marisa and a playpen for the boys here in the family room so we can hear them if they need us."

Pete came over to take Marisa and put her in her crib. Jim came to get the boys, followed by Alex.

Tabitha stared at Alex, wondering what he was doing, but he offered to take Tommy from Evelyn, and the baby acted as if he knew him. He carried the little boy just as Jim carried Johnny and put him down on his tummy in the playpen.

"Where did you learn about babies?" Tabitha asked.

"Today at Jim's. He showed me." Alex grinned at her. "Were you impressed?"

"Yes, I was."

He offered her his arm. "May I escort you to dinner?"

She stood, but she held him back as the others moved to the buffet spread out on the kitchen counter.

"Why are you here, Alex?" she whispered. "What was so urgent that you had to bother Jim this afternoon?"

"Nothing urgent…exactly. I just wanted to see you, make sure you got back all right."

"Mona said she'd tell you if I didn't."

"I know." The others were concentrating on filling their plates and Alex leaned down. "But she couldn't tell me this." Then he kissed her.

Tabitha jumped back as if he'd bitten her. "Don't do that!"

"Why?"

She stared at him as if he were a lunatic. "Because of Jenny, of course!"

"Come on, guys," Pete called out. "As host, I have to go last, and I'm starving."

"After you," Alex said, waving Tabitha in front of him.

Tabitha had no choice unless she wanted to make a scene, and that was the last thing she wanted to do. She filled her plate with brisket, potato salad, green beans and coleslaw. Then she went into the dining room.

"Here, Tabitha," Evelyn called out. "We saved two seats for you and Alex."

Tabitha wanted to groan, but she could only smile and nod her gratitude. She took the seat next to Evelyn, leaving the last seat next to Jim for Alex. She hoped she could keep Evelyn from asking any difficult questions of Alex.

But she doubted it.

The evening was typical for their family, but Tabitha saw it tonight through Alex's eyes. She knew he was enjoying himself. It was on his face. And he clearly got on well with her brothers-in-law. Even Joel seemed to approve of Alex.

When dinner was over, they all pitched in to clean up and store away the extra food.

"I'll fix some decaf to go with dessert," Tommie said. "By the time it's ready, the kitchen will be cleaned. What did you bring for dessert, Teresa?"

"Jim insisted on an ice cream cake. He loves those."

"Who doesn't?" Joel asked.

"I've never had one," Alex admitted. "What are they like?"

"Oh, they're the best. Layers of ice cream and cake. It's wonderful," Teresa explained, making it clear she loved them too.

"Well, I think that description will make me work harder to get things cleaned up," Alex said, loading the dishwasher.

"You must clean up a lot. You're doing a great job loading the dishwasher," Tommie said.

"I used to work in a restaurant."

"I was told he's an excellent chef, too," Tabitha added, deciding he should suffer a little.

"What can you cook?" Pete asked.

"Mostly Italian," Alex admitted.

"Italian? Myerson? That doesn't sound Italian," Jim pointed out.

"My godfather is Italian," Alex said, winking at Tabitha. "He taught me to cook."

"Well, the next family gathering, you're the chef," Pete said. "I love Italian!"

"Just name the time and place. I'd love to cook for everyone. I owe you for this delightful evening,"

There was a sudden silence as they realized Alex was serious. Finally, Jim slapped him on the shoulder. "Man, we've got to get you out more. This is just normal stuff. You don't owe us anything."

"Yes, I do," Alex said quietly.

Tabitha's heart hurt. After having met his parents, she knew exactly what Alex meant. The warmth and love were easily given among her family tonight. She hadn't seen an ounce of it when she'd met Mr. and Mrs. Myerson.

* * *

When the evening ended, and Alex realized she'd ridden with her mother and Joel, he asked to take her home.

"It's not necessary. I'm on their way and—"

"Tabitha, I need to talk to you."

"We don't have anything to talk about, Alex. There's—"

Instead of listening to her, Alex turned to Joel. "Is it all right if I take Tabitha home?"

"It's fine with us if it's okay with Tabitha," Joel assured him.

Tabitha was fighting an inner war. She knew she didn't need to be alone with Alex. But she wanted to talk to him, to hear what the people in Detroit had said, how he'd enjoyed the evening, what was happening with his book. The gentle look in his eyes made it impossible to refuse.

"Yes, that's fine, Joel. Thanks for bringing me."

"No problem. Good night."

They all said their goodbyes and Tabitha went down the sidewalk with Alex to a black Mercedes.

"This is your car?" she asked.

"Yeah. Is there a problem?"

"No, of course not. It's very nice."

He opened the door for her and she slid into the comfortable leather seat. After closing the door, he walked around to get behind the steering wheel. "Where do I go?" he asked.

"Turn right at the corner," she began, following with directions to her condo.

They didn't speak during the drive and Tabitha wasn't sure why he'd insisted on driving her home. She'd had a lot she'd wanted to ask him, too, but somehow she couldn't bring herself to start a conversation.

When they reached her condo, he pulled into her driveway and turned off the motor.

"There's no need for you to get out, Alex. I'll be fine."

"I thought maybe we could talk for a little while."

"I—I suppose we could. What did they say when you called Detroit?"

"I talked to both men, and they're growing close and sharing a lot of things. They've done a couple of segments on Daniel's show and they've gone over well. The station is fielding a lot of calls wanting more information."

"That's wonderful."

"Yeah. And Bill asked again if you were interested in a job with them. I told him you were all booked up."

"Thanks."

Silence grew between them.

"You certainly learned to handle a baby quickly," Tabitha finally said. "I didn't think you'd had any experience with them."

"I hadn't," Alex admitted with a grin. "But when Jim answered the door, he was trying to bathe the babies and get them dressed before he fed them. I didn't actually bathe them, but I dried them off and diapered them and dressed them. Which was harder than it sounds because their arms and legs are going in all different directions at once."

"I'm sure," she said, grinning.

"But Jim was a good teacher. And he trusted me."

"I noticed you got along well with him and Pete."

"Yeah. They're great guys."

"Yes, they are."

More silence.

"Our families are quite different, aren't they?" Alex said quietly.

She nodded. "I'm glad you got to meet mine."

"Me, too. I've never met a real family like that."

She didn't argue with him. Jenny had had no family, and he might as well not have had any.

"Are they like that all the time?"

Tabitha turned to look at him. "If you're asking if tonight was unusual, no, it wasn't."

"I didn't think so."

"As you saw, we're not big cooks. Mom held down a job while we were growing up and we learned the basics. Teresa's the best, but she doesn't have the time now with the twins. Still, I'm sure you could cook circles around any of us."

"That doesn't matter, honey. The food was good. It doesn't matter who fixed it."

"It was an issue with Pete for a while, when he and Tommie began dating. He was old-fashioned and had made up his mind that he would have a stay-at-home wife who could prepare dinner parties with almost no notice and keep the house spotless and have lots of children."

"What tree was he living in?" Alex asked with a grin.

"I know. Tommie just told him that wasn't happening. He finally decided he needed Tommie more than the perfect housekeeper. So they get by with spaghetti and meat loaf, and when they have the family over they bring food in.

"Jim and Teresa were already expecting twins when they got married. They've had us over a couple of times. Teresa makes a great chicken parmigiano. You'd like it."

"Do you ever have them over?"

"I've had them over a couple of times, but I don't have much room. And now, with the babies, I'm not sure what we'd do. I guess I need to find a bigger place, now that I can afford it, but I hate moving."

"Yeah. I need a new house, too."

"You do? But that's the house you shared with Jenny, isn't it?"

"Yeah."

"Why are you moving out of it?"

"I rattle around in it. We bought it because she wanted it and intended to fill it with kids. But after she died, there was just me."

"So you're going to move somewhere smaller?"

"I don't know. I liked Jim and Teresa's house. And Pete and Tommie's, too. That neighborhood would be good."

"Where do you live now?"

When he told her his address, she recognized his neighborhood, one known for its huge houses and wealthy owners who were the movers and shakers of Fort Worth. Tabitha stared at him. "Why would you want to sell your house there and move to Jim and Pete's area?"

"My neighborhood doesn't have a lot of families in it."

"But you don't have a family."

"No. But I might have one someday." He smiled at her, but Tabitha continued to stare.

"Don't you believe me?" he asked.

Truthfully, when it came to Alex, she didn't know what to believe.

Chapter Twelve

The next morning, Alex began preparing lunch, determined to impress Tabitha. He'd convinced her last night to come see his house, to give him her opinion.

Then he figured he'd get her to help him pick out a new house in the neighborhood where her sisters lived. He was prepared to take awhile to convince her that he loved her. But he wasn't going to give up.

When the doorbell sounded, Alex did one final check of the table. Then he hurried to the door. "Right on time, Tabitha. Come in."

"Thanks." She looked around as she stepped in. "Your house is an absolute palace, Alex."

"Yeah, but it's not what I want."

"So why did you buy it?"

"Jenny enjoyed showing off our wealth. That's one of those things I try to forget."

"It's not such a bad sin," Tabitha told him.

With a sigh, he said, "Well, it did give me a good kitchen."

She nodded, but said nothing else.

"Come sit down. Lunch is ready," Alex said abruptly.

Tabitha followed him into the breakfast room, which was as big as her living room. He pulled out a chair for her and then sat across from her.

They started with a salad that Tabitha really enjoyed. Then Alex served her chicken alfredo. It was delicious.

"Did you make this yourself?" she asked.

"Of course I did. Think it's good enough to make for the family?"

"Yes, of course it is, but it's not necessary for you to cook for my family."

"So you think I'd be…overstepping my bounds?"

"No, that's not what I meant, Alex. But you don't owe them anything."

"Why not? They welcomed me last night. I ate their food, shared their time. I always understood that you repaid people by inviting them to your place."

"But if you're going to sell this house, then you need to wait until you have a new house. Then you could invite everyone over so they'd know how to find you."

Tabitha's cell phone rang before Alex could respond.

"Excuse me," she said and answered her phone.

After a few minutes, she said, "It's Jim. He wants to talk to you."

Alex took the phone from her and spoke to Jim.

Tabitha sat there, wanting him to accept the invitation from her brother-in-law because she didn't think

Alex had made many friends. And not wanting him to because if he was constantly around her family, she'd suffer.

"Thanks, Jim, that'd be great. Bye."

He handed the phone back to Tabitha. "That's really nice of Jim."

"What?"

"Didn't he tell you? He got his company's Ranger tickets and he and Pete and Joel are going tonight. But they had a fourth ticket and thought I might like to go."

"Oh, that is nice. So you're a baseball fan?"

"Not exactly. I've never been to a game, but I thought it might be fun."

"I'm sure it will be."

After lunch, he showed Tabitha through the house. Sadly, he only lived on the first floor. The second story was empty, as was half of the first floor, too. He'd moved out of the master bedroom when Jenny died. Tabitha thought the bedroom he lived in was one intended for the housekeeper.

"You don't have a housekeeper?"

"I have a lady who cleans a couple of days a week. That's all."

"Where's your office?"

"Not here. I have an office near Harris Hospital."

"Well, you certainly have a lot of space here that you're not using."

"Yeah. Do you think Tommie would list it for me?"

"I'm sure she will, but this really isn't her area. You might be better off listing it with someone who specializes in this area."

"And I think I should list it with Tommie. When is she going back to work?"

"Not for a couple of months."

"Hmmm. I'll have to talk to her."

"Alex, why are you really selling your house?"

"I told you, honey. Jenny was my past. I want a future."

"I don't believe you."

"Why not?"

"Because every time I touched you, no matter how innocently, you jerked away."

"That was true at first. But the night we looked at the baby's pictures, you were the one who jerked away."

She didn't like him pointing that out. "Of course I did. Only a masochist would try to have a relationship with a man who is still in love with his dead wife."

"But I'm not."

"I don't believe you."

He stared at her before he said, "What can I do to show you?"

"You—you could kiss me. That would be a start."

Alex let a smile play about his lips. She'd given him the answer he wanted. "Gladly." He pulled her into his arms and lowered his mouth to hers.

The hunger that grew in him ensured that he didn't pull away until Tabitha was truly kissed. In fact, he pulled her more tightly against him, enjoying the feel of her slim body against his. He lifted his lips and reslanted them across Tabitha's mouth, to take her deeper. His hunger grew every minute.

When Tabitha tried to pull back, Alex held her tightly against him, telling himself it was only because he wanted to convince her. Truthfully it was because of the desire she stirred in him. He had to let her go before he took her right there on the floor.

"Sorry," he said, short of breath. "I—I got a little carried away."

She stared at him, wide-eyed, as if in shock.

"Honey, are you all right? Did I hurt you?"

She shook her head, but suddenly she needed to get out of his house, away from him. She began backing toward the door.

"Where are you going?"

"Home. I'm going home."

"Don't you want to take your purse and keys with you?"

She grabbed them out of his hand and turned and ran out of the house to her car.

Alex watched her drive away, hoping she didn't have a wreck. Somehow, he'd thought things would happen differently.

While the men enjoyed the baseball game, the ladies all came to Teresa's house for dessert.

"Was Alex happy about going to the game?" Tommie asked.

"Yes, but he's never been to a game before." Tabitha was still recovering from her visit to Alex's home. "Uh, I saw his house today. He wanted to know if you'd list it for him, but I said he should get someone who specializes in his neighborhood. Is that all right?"

"Of course it is. But actually he talked to me the other night about listing his house. I told him I list homes in all areas. Where is it located?"

When Tabitha told her, Tommie's eyes widened. "Wow! It must be an expensive home."

"It's a palace," Tabitha said, part of the emotion in her words coming from the events there that day rather than the house itself.

"How big is it?" Teresa asked.

"Huge. None of the second-story rooms is occupied, and only half of the ground floor. I think he sleeps in the maid's room. He moved out of the master bedroom after Jenny died."

"How long ago did she die?" Tommie asked.

"It was a year the day we left for the tour. He was quite disagreeable that day."

"But he seems to have adjusted since then."

"Sort of." Tabitha still wasn't quite sure if this morning meant he was over mourning for Jenny, or if he was just trying to prove a point. As much as she would enjoy being with Alex, she had a fear that he would change his mind the next day, as he had on the tour. As intensely as he'd loved Jenny, she was sure it would take years for him to recover.

"Well, I'm glad he gets along well with my boys. They all seem to enjoy each other," Evelyn said, a smile on her lips.

"But he may not— I mean, he has his own life."

Evelyn stared at Tabitha. "Oh, I'm sorry, dear. I thought they invited him because of you. You mean you don't feel anything for him?"

Tabitha sat there, unable to answer Evelyn.

Ann answered instead. "She and Alex are friends, Evelyn, but we'll have to see what happens after they've become better acquainted with each other."

Tabitha gave her mother a grateful smile.

"So you think his house is worth half a million?" Tommie asked, clearly still intrigued by the idea of listing it.

"I would guess double that, Tommie, but I'm not the expert. I think they bought it new when they got married."

"Oh, mercy, that would be a nice maternity-leave payment."

Teresa said, "If you need me to keep Marisa while you visit his house, I'll be glad to do so."

"Or I could," Tabitha said, "if you leave me instructions."

Teresa grinned. "Hey, we could do that together. It would be fun."

"Oh, yes, I'd like that." Tabitha agreed.

"How about tomorrow?" Tommie asked.

Both sisters agreed.

"Great. I need to strike while the iron is hot."

"Tomorrow is Saturday," Evelyn pointed out. "I could baby-sit if you girls want to go somewhere."

"Thanks, Evelyn, but Tabitha and I will enjoy it."

A night out with the guys.

That was a new experience for Alex. He had gone out with friends occasionally when he was younger, but not lately.

Jim was providing instructions about watching a ball game, helped occasionally by Joel and Pete. They all jumped to their feet and cheered when the Rangers hit a homer that tied the score.

"I should've watched baseball before," Alex said. "It's a good way to release tension."

"You've got tension?" Pete asked.

"Yeah, a little. I tried to convince Tabitha I'm not still mourning my wife and…it didn't go so well."

"What did you try?"

"I asked her how I could prove that I was no longer mourning my wife, and she suggested I kiss her."

Even Joel turned to stare at Alex. "Why would she ask that?"

"On the tour, I told her I didn't like to be touched. I kissed her once and then jerked away. She wouldn't come near me again after that."

"So did you pass the test?" Pete asked.

"I passed it so well, I think I scared her a little."

"What did she do?" Joel asked, concern in his voice.

"She stared at me and said nothing. Then she basically ran to her car."

"Did you call to see if she got home safely?"

"I still don't have her number," Alex said in disgust. "You'd think I'd remember to get it before I made her mad."

Joel pulled out a pen and paper and wrote something down. "Here you go. You've earned it."

Alex looked at the paper and discovered a telephone number on it. "Tabitha's?" he asked eagerly.

"Yeah. But don't tell her where you got it."

"No, Joel, I won't. But thank you so much."

"Glad to do it. You'd fit in well in our family."

Pete nodded at Alex. "Yeah, Joel's right."

"If only we got to make the decision," Jim added. "Some of the guys Tabitha has brought around worried me. We wanted someone who would fit with us."

"Why would she bring that kind of man around?"

"They're all beautiful ladies. But with her videos, I think Tabitha drew the wrong type of men." Pete looked at his brother and Joel. "At least that was my take on it. I knew Tommie and Teresa wouldn't be getting a divorce, but I feared for Tabitha."

"I can promise I won't divorce her, if I can ever convince her to marry me." Alex stared off into the distance, as if he were seeing the future.

"That's what we like to hear," Joel assured him.

About that time the Rangers got another hit and the four men leaped to their feet to cheer.

When the game was over, they got in Pete's car and headed back to his house. Tommie was watching for them and came running out as the men got out of the car.

"Alex, are you sure you want me to list your house?" she asked.

"Yes, I'm sure. Did you think I was joking?"

"I hope not. A house like yours would be a major sale for me."

"Good."

"Will it be all right if I come tomorrow to look at it?"

"Sure. Maybe Tabitha will come with you."

"No, she's going to take care of Marisa at Teresa's house," Tommie said without concern.

"Hey, wait a minute. She hasn't spent much time with Marisa," Pete protested.

"No one has spent much time with her, including you. But I thought you might want to go with me tomorrow."

"Oh, I hadn't thought of that. Is it okay with you, Alex?"

"Of course, Pete. Any of you can come."

"I can't," Joel said at once. "Ann worked all week. Saturday is our day together."

"I'd better stay home with the baby-sitters. That way, there will be three adults for three babies." Jim grinned at the others. "It's not easy to manage twins by oneself."

"You're a good dad, Jim. I hope I'm as good when my turn comes."

"So you want children?" Joel asked.

"Yes, of course."

"Good. That will please Ann. And me too." Joel couldn't hold back a grin.

"Yeah. Now all I have to do is convince Tabitha."

Teresa showed Tabitha how to care for Marisa and the boys. The newest baby still had the umbilical cord attached to her belly button, but Teresa assured her sister that was perfectly normal.

After they got all three down for a nap, they relaxed in the family room while Jim made sandwiches.

"So, are you convinced you want a baby?" Teresa asked Tabitha.

"Definitely. All I have to do is find a daddy for it."

"Are you sure you haven't done that already?" Jim asked, coming into the room with two plates. He gave one each to the ladies before he headed back to the kitchen to get his.

"What do you mean, Jim?" Teresa asked as he sat down next to her.

"Yes, I'd like to know that, too." Tabitha stared at him.

"It was just a thought. Alex seems interested in having a family." Jim took a big bite of his sandwich.

"I don't see how Alex's wishes have any connection to mine," Tabitha said, staring rigidly ahead.

"You mean he *didn't* pass the test?" Jim asked in surprise.

Tabitha felt her cheeks flush. "He told you? How dare he do that!"

"Wait a minute. What test are we talking about?" Teresa demanded.

Jim looked at Tabitha. She finally muttered, "I told him to kiss me because he's always drawn back whenever I touched him. Well, almost always."

"So did he?" Teresa asked. "Did he pass the test?"

Tabitha nodded.

"Well, then, what's the trouble? You love him. He loves you. That works for me."

"You don't understand. That doesn't mean he's over Jenny. In fact, I don't think he'll ever be over Jenny."

"But what if you're wrong?" Jim asked. "He sounded like he wants a future with you."

"I—I think he's confused."

Teresa leaned over to her. "Maybe you are, too."

"Teresa," Tommie said through the phone, "is Tabitha still there?"

"Of course she is."

"Well, Alex wants her to see the house he's found. Can you and Jim manage all three babies for half an hour?"

"Of course we can. When will you be here?"

"In about fifteen minutes. What? Oh, Pete says he'll stay and help with Marisa."

"No need. We'll manage. All three are asleep right now."

"Okay, we'll be there in a few minutes."

Teresa stopped Jim as he was going past her. "Alex is coming to get Tabitha to get her to look at a house he wants to buy."

"Think she'll go with him?"

"I didn't think of that! Do you think she will?"

"Well, it might require him taking another test," Jim said with a grin.

"Oh, I bet he'd hate that." Teresa laughed before she asked, "Should we warn her?"

"I don't think so. Where is she, anyway?"

"She thought she heard Marisa cry, so she went to check on her."

Marisa had awakened and Tabitha changed her diaper and wrapped her back in her pink blanket and brought her to the family room.

"Is it time to feed her again?"

Teresa checked her watch. "Yes, I believe so. I'll fix her bottle."

Tabitha sat in the rocker, softly talking to the baby, who stared at her as if hanging on her every word.

Teresa came back with the bottle.

"Should we wait until she fusses?" Tabitha asked.

"Probably." Teresa cocked her head to one side. "I

think someone is here. Maybe they're here to pick up Marisa."

The doorbell rang and Jim answered it. "Hi, guys. Did you finish looking at Alex's house?"

Tommie gave him a sharp look but played along. "Yes, but Alex wants to see a house in our neighborhood and he thought Tabitha might like to see it, too."

"Ah. Well, come on in and we'll ask her."

But Tabitha said no, there was no need for her to go.

"Yes, there is, honey," Alex said.

"No, there's not."

"Yes, there is. I'm buying this house so we can live there and raise our children there. I think you should have a vote, don't you?"

"Alex, you can't— We're not— This is ridiculous!"

He put his arms around her. "Just come with me for a few minutes. You're not committing yourself to anything, I promise."

She looked around at her family's eager faces. "All right. But who will take care of Marisa? The boys are due to wake up soon."

"I'm staying here to take care of my daughter," Pete said.

Soon they were all back in Pete's car, Tommie driving. They only went a couple of streets over, between Tommie's house and Teresa's. There was a new house just finished that had a for sale sign in the front yard.

"This house? But it's not nearly as large as your house," Tabitha said.

"I know. I told you my house was too big. But this one has enough room and a big kitchen, Tommie said."

Tommie turned to look at Alex. "Why do you need a big kitchen?"

"So I can cook," Alex said.

"Wow. That's the right answer, isn't it, Tabitha?"

Tabitha said nothing. When Tommie parked the car, she slid out of the back seat, determined not to show any appreciation for the house.

Tommie went to the door and opened the lock box. Then she unlocked the door. "This house is going on the weekly tour next week. You're getting a chance to see it early."

She swung back the front door and led the way in. Alex grabbed Tabitha's hand as they walked through the door. It was a one-story house, Tabitha noted. It would be a nice home for someone.

"Nice entry," Alex said.

"Here's the living room on the right and the dining room on the left. Do you want to go through the dining room to the kitchen first?"

"Yeah, I think so," Alex agreed.

The kitchen was beautiful, even Tabitha admitted that. The family room was a nice size, but still warm and charming. It had a fireplace, too. Tabitha could picture a fire burning on a cold winter night and a couple cuddling on the sofa in front of it. Alex squeezed her hand, as if he'd read her mind.

She tried to pull her hand loose, but he wouldn't let go.

The study was definitely masculine, but still attractive. Then they reached the master bedroom. Tabitha couldn't hold back a sigh. It was heavenly, and the bath connected to it was huge. The other bedrooms were nice, too, though they didn't compare to the master.

They came back into the living room.

"What do you think, Tabitha?" Alex asked softly.

"It's—it's very nice."

"I like it. Is there anything about it you don't like?"

"No, but my opinion doesn't matter!"

"Yes, it does. I passed the test, remember?"

"Alex! I can't believe you told them!"

"I'm desperate. I've fallen in love with you, Tabitha. I want to have a future with only you."

"You're just saying that," she said with a sniff.

"No, sweetheart, I'm not. You brought me back to life on the tour. By the time we ended it, I knew I didn't want to be without you. But I'd done such a good job convincing you I would never let Jenny go, that you wouldn't believe me."

"But, Alex, I—"

"Let's try that test again."

"But Tommie's—"

Alex ignored her protest and pulled her into his arms, his lips coaxing hers. Before she knew it, Tabitha was swept away to a private island where she was completely surrounded by Alex. His touch warmed her like the heat of the tropical sun, and his lips swept over her like the flowing tide.

The kiss was everything she'd ever wanted from Alex, and yet it was only the beginning. She never wanted it to end.

When Alex shifted his lips to get air, Tabitha couldn't

hold back the words that spilled from her mouth. "Poor Jenny. I—"

Alex, intent on resuming the kiss, muttered, "Who?"

Instantly Tabitha pulled back and stared into his eyes.

"What's the matter, Tabitha? Did I do something wrong?"

Wrong? Not at all, she thought. But still she was so shocked, she had to question him. "I said Jenny's name, but you—you didn't recognize who I was talking about."

"That's because I was concentrating on you, Tabitha. It's not that I forgot who Jenny was, but you were the woman in my thoughts. In my arms." He cradled her face in his two hands. "Why are you so surprised? I tried to tell you I wanted a future with you."

"I know, but—but I didn't believe you."

"Do you believe me now?"

"Yes, I believe you," Tabitha said in a wonder-filled voice. "And I accept your proposal, Alex. If you're sure."

He lifted her up and spun her around, and Tabitha had her answer. A huge smile lit up his face, and he verified her assumption. "I couldn't be more sure." And then he kissed her again.

Tabitha's heart was about to burst, she was so happy. But there were things that needed to be said. She pulled back from Alex and told him, "I want you to understand that it's not that I don't want you to talk about Jenny if you need to. She'll always be a part of you, I know that."

"She will, Tabitha. But you're my future."

Tabitha rose up on her toes and initiated a kiss. Her

arms wound around his neck and pulled him down to her mouth; she let her lips tell him how happy she was.

"Do I take it you want the house, then?"

At the sound of Tommie's voice, they both turned to her, amusement on their faces.

"I think it's perfect." Alex looked down at Tabitha with a question in his eyes.

Tabitha nodded and smiled. "I can already see our children running through it," she said, pulling him down for another taste.

Tommie coughed and said, "We'd better get out of here before you start making those kids tonight!"

Once again, Tabitha was on the flight home from a tour. Her client, an agreeable woman with a cookbook to promote, was sitting beside her.

"I'm glad the tour is over. You did a fine job, Tabitha, but I miss home."

"I understand. We'll be landing in about fifteen minutes. Are you sure I don't need to take you to your door?"

"No, my husband is meeting me. He missed me," she said with a satisfied smile.

Tabitha knew what she meant. Alex had called her every night while she was gone. She'd gone to sleep with him in her mind and heart. She knew her capitulation had seemed fast, especially to her mom, but she'd fallen in love with Alex on the tour. When she'd finally realized he loved her, too, she couldn't see any need to resist.

She'd done something while she was in New York

that might displease Alex. She'd called his parents and told them she and Alex were marrying. She'd even invited them to the wedding, which was planned for a week from today.

Her sisters and her mother and even Evelyn were all helping her get ready for the wedding. She'd found a bridal gown before she went on tour. A cake had been ordered, and refreshments planned. Her pastor had agreed to do the ceremony at their new house.

Alex had already bought the house. Since he was paying cash, there was little delay. Tommie had already found a buyer for his old house, so things were moving swiftly.

When she came up the walkway from the plane, she saw Alex waiting for her. She took a deep breath and hurried forward, eager to feel his arms around her.

"Welcome home," he whispered before he kissed her.

"You haven't changed your mind?" she asked, staring at him.

"No, sweetheart, I haven't changed my mind." After he kissed her again, he whispered, "Have you?"

She shook her head.

"What's wrong?" he asked, seeing something in her manner that worried him.

"I'll—I'll tell you once we're alone."

There was no conversation until they reached Alex's car. Once they were inside, shut off from the rest of the world, she said, "I called your parents. I invited them to the wedding."

He studied her for a few minutes. Then he calmly said, "Why did you do that?"

"Because I wanted them to have the opportunity to join us if they chose to do so. If they don't come, we haven't lost anything."

"True," he said with a lopsided grin.

"I'm hoping they realize what they have already lost. You're such a special person, Alex. They have every reason to be proud of you."

"Sweetheart, you might be just a little bit prejudiced," he said with another smile.

"Maybe, but I think I'm right. So, do you forgive me?"

"Always. But if they come, you'll have to entertain them. I'm no good at it."

"Maybe you just need practice," she suggested with a big smile.

The day before the wedding, Tabitha got a phone call from Alex's mother, asking if she could make them a reservation for a hotel room. Tabitha agreed at once, picking a nice hotel near their neighborhood. When she invited them to join the wedding-rehearsal dinner party that night, though, she was politely turned down.

"Baby steps," she reminded herself. She wanted to give Alex a sense of his own family. But no matter what, he was getting a family. He and Jim and Pete were great together. That was very important to Tabitha because she and her sisters liked to be together.

They'd also discussed starting a family.

"Will you mind having a baby soon?" Alex asked. "I don't want it to interfere too much in your career."

Tabitha pursed her lips and then asked, "Is my having a career important to you?"

"Me? Absolutely not. But I want you to be happy."

"I can continue to work on my videos, but I'd love to start a family as soon as possible."

"Mmm, how about tonight?" Alex suggested, lifting one eyebrow.

"Absolutely not. I promised my mother I wouldn't get pregnant until after I was married," she assured him primly.

Alex laughed. "I guess I can wait until tomorrow. But then we're going to get busy."

"Perfect. Oh, I forgot to tell you, your parents are coming in for the wedding."

Alex stared at her. "I don't believe you."

"It's true. Your mother called and asked me to make a hotel reservation for them. I asked them to come tonight to the rehearsal dinner, but she thought they might be tired."

"Okay, sweetheart, you win. I never thought for a minute they'd come. Obviously, you're more persuasive than I am."

Tabitha put her arms around her future husband's neck. "I think they didn't realize it would matter. But I think they might change a little if we make sure they feel welcome."

"I love an optimistic wife," he said before he kissed her.

"Hey, you two, we're here to rehearse. You need to save that until tomorrow," Pete called as he and Tommie came through the door.

"Spoilsport!" Alex said with a grin. "Where's the rest of the family?"

"They're right behind us, and the preacher is behind them. Is everything ready?"

"I hope so. They set up the chairs in the living room and the altar is finished and the flowers in place."

"Heck, I don't care about flowers and candles. I want to know about the rehearsal dinner. I'm starving!"

Tommie slapped her husband's arm. "Behave yourself, Pete."

"Not to worry. I'm the elder statesman, the oldest son-in-law in terms of seniority. If they start getting rid of sons-in-law, I'll be the last to go!"

"Well, don't look at me! I'm not going anywhere," Alex assured him.

The two men were laughing and teasing each other. Tommie stepped to Tabitha's side. "I think you found the third twin, sister. You'd think they were kin except that Alex's hair is lighter."

"I know. I'm so pleased that they get along well."

Then everyone was there and Evelyn, who had assumed the role of wedding coordinator, had them lined up and going through their paces.

The pastor explained how he handled the ceremony, repeating the words that Tabitha and Alex would say.

When they were finished, Alex sent everyone to the buffet set up in the kitchen by the caterers. As they all rushed in that direction, Alex caught Tabitha's hand.

She turned and looked at him. "Aren't you hungry?"

"More than you know, sweetheart. I have something I want to give you." He handed her a box with a big bow.

"But we're exchanging our presents tomorrow, aren't we?"

"This is an extra present."

"Wasn't my ring enough?" He'd given her a beautiful diamond engagement ring.

"I want to give you the world, but for now, accept this."

She opened the box, unsure what to expect. Inside she found a sheet of paper, a dedication for his new book.

This book is dedicated to my beloved wife, Tabitha Tyler Myerson, who taught me to live again after a devastating loss. She brought joy back into my life and led me to appreciate the gifts God has given to us.

As she read the words, Tabitha's eyes filled with tears. Through them she looked up at her future husband. "Thank you, Alex. This is a very special gift."

"Not nearly as special as you, my love." And then he took her in his arms and kissed her again before they joined their family.

* * * * *

SILHOUETTE *Romance*®

Christmas comes to

HARLEQUIN ROMANCE®

In November 2005, don't miss:

MISTLETOE MARRIAGE
(#3869)

by Jessica Hart

For Sophie Beckwith, this Christmas means
facing the ex who dumped her and then married
her sister! Only one person can help: her best friend
Bram. Bram used to be engaged to Sophie's sister,
and now, determined to show the lovebirds that
they've moved on, he's come up with a plan: he's
proposed to Sophie!

Then in December look out for:

CHRISTMAS GIFT: A FAMILY
(#3873)

by Barbara Hannay

Happy with his life as a wealthy bachelor,
Hugh Strickland is stunned to discover he has
a daughter. He wants to bring Ivy home—but he's
absolutely terrified! Hugh hardly knows Jo Berry,
but he pleads with her to help him—surely the ideal
solution would be to give each other the perfect
Christmas gift: a family....

Available wherever Harlequin books are sold.

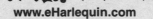

HRXMAS

SILHOUETTE *Romance*

COMING NEXT MONTH

#1790 TAMING OF THE TWO—Elizabeth Harbison
Shakespeare in Love

Beyond old-fashioned, Kate Gregory's father is *ancient*-fashioned and insists she find a man so that her younger sister can marry! Not liking *that* ultimatum, Kate secretly enlists the help of her childhood nemesis, Ben Devere. And it's not long before their pretend scenario has Kate thinking that Father just might know best!

#1791 SNOWBOUND BABY—Susan Meier
Bryant Baby Bonanza

Desperate to deliver a check that would save his ranch, the last place Cooper Bryant needed to be was stranded in a blizzard with a beautiful stranger and her baby. As he gets to know his reluctant housemate during cozy fireside chats, Cooper begins reassessing his priorities. But once this interlude ends, will Cooper sacrifice everything for the love that will save *him* from himself?

#1792 HIS SLEEPING BEAUTY—Carol Grace
Fairy-Tale Brides

Sarah Jennings leads a protected, isolated life. Until the night she is caught sleepwalking in her relative's garden and rescued by her handsome, cynical next-door neighbor. But as her midnight rescuer's kisses awaken Sarah from her slumber, will Max Monroe's teachings help her embrace life…and his love?

#1793 THE MARINE AND ME—Cathie Linz

When U.S. Marine Captain Steve Kozlowski learns that Chloe Johnson is a far cry from the frumpy librarian he'd presumed her to be, he feels betrayed by her previous presentation. But as the two pair up to outwit her matchmaking grandmother, Steve's attraction to her has him contemplating his most challenging tour of duty—matrimony!

SRCNM1005